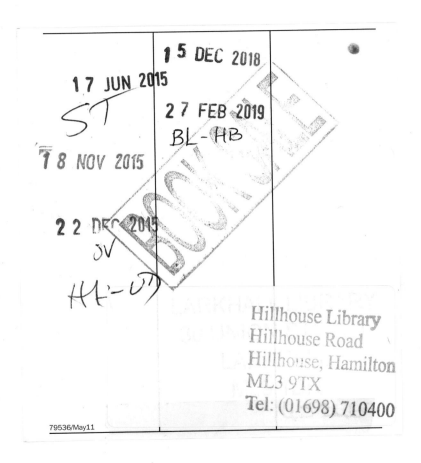

Old Guns

July 1892

Whilst still recovering from the death of his old partner, Abner, Sam Ransom learns of a note, left by the dead man, warning that the infamous Meak twins are after Ransom's life because of what happened at Bur Oak Springs almost two decades ago. Ransom knows he must alert the rest of his gang who were there.

Bur Oak Springs was a ghost-town even then, but now Ransom's family is in jeopardy and their only hope of salvation is the gang's return to confront the Meak brothers in a battle fraught with a sense of déjà-vu.

It's going to be a bloody showdown: young guns against the old.

By the same author

Death at Bethesda Falls
Last Chance Saloon
The $300 Man
Blind Justice at Wedlock

Old Guns

Ross Morton

A Black Horse Western

ROBERT HALE · LONDON

© Ross Morton 2011
First published in Great Britain 2012

ISBN 978-0-7090-9380-0

Robert Hale Limited
Clerkenwell House
Clerkenwell Green
London EC1R 0HT

www.halebooks.com

The right of Ross Morton to be identified as
author of this work has been asserted by him
in accordance with the Copyright, Designs and
Patents Act 1988

To Jennifer, my wife and best friend, Hannah,
Harry and Darius
And thanks to Tony Masero

1892

PROLOGUE

PENITENTIARY

Monday, 4 July

'Thanks for seeing me, Warden,' Justus Meak said as he stopped in front of the prison administrator's desk. Despite the predatory aspect of the prisoner's beaked nose and bristling whiskers, there appeared to be sincerity in his tarnished-penny eyes. Behind Justus stood the bulk of Guard Seers, truncheon at the ready, florid pockmarked face impassive. Meak's long brown hair covered his ears and hung lank and damp. Dark patches of sweat discoloured both men's clothes and their flushed faces ran in unsightly beads.

'It's my job, Meak.' Warden Trent removed his spectacles, put them on the desk and used a large grey handkerchief to wipe his brow and eyes. He shifted his overweight bulk in his seat. The damnable weather was hot and humid and he was grossly uncomfortable. The air was still and oppressive and the entire prison smelled. He leaned his elbows on the inlaid leather top and steepled his big hands. 'You had bad news in the mail, I believe?'

'Yes, sir.' Justus thrust out his pointed chin. 'It's our ma, she's dying.' He fished in his pocket and thrust forward the letter, the chains of his manacles clinking.

Warden Trent took the sheet but didn't bother to read its scrawl. As a matter of course, all mail was opened and read before being passed to the inmates. He reckoned that he understood why, of the two brothers, Justus elected to come today. The bad news might have been too much for his twin Gideon, who was rumoured to possess a short temper. Though, to be fair, Justus managed to keep him in check. As far as he knew, they'd both toed the line throughout their sentence.

'Ma asks if we can go see her so she can pass away happy.'

'Aye, I can understand her grief at having her only two boys locked up.' Trent shook his head and grimaced, the dampness of his collar quite irritating. 'Maybe you should have thought about the consequences of your actions before you robbed the bank.'

'I know, sir, but we're all she's got . . . It's our Ma.'

'I sympathize.' Trent shuffled papers in front of him; some of them blotched by sweat from his own forehead. There were precedents on compassionate grounds, he knew. 'But you've still got two years to serve before you'll even be considered for parole.'

Justus leaned forward, his manacled hands lifted in prayer fashion in front of him. Guard Seers took a step closer, his truncheon ready, but Trent waved him back.

'Can't you send a deputy with us, Warden?' Justus pleaded, his face all twisted.

6

Trent rose from his desk and paced to the only window in his office. Hands clasped behind his back, he felt the sweat soak into his pants waistband. He peered through the bars at the exercise yard. He'd given orders that the inmates could spend longer outside, as the cells were insufferably hot. Prisoners in traditional grey garb milled around, shiftless as they hugged the shade cast by the wall. They all looked like lost souls. Mothers' sons, every one, of course. He'd have liked to say farewell to his mother, but he'd been in the thick of fighting in the Wilderness when she passed away. Shrugging off his maudlin thoughts, Trent turned. 'You've both been model prisoners, Meak, I'll grant you that.'

'Yes, sir.' Meak nodded. 'And we deeply regret what we've done. We truly want to mend our ways.'

'You can save that spiel, son, I'm not the parole board.' Trent eyed the desk calendar, his mind made up. 'Very well, as an Independence Day concession you and your brother can go visit your mother. I'll send Deputy Stone along with you tomorrow.'

'Thank you, Warden.'

It was a risk, but he'd warn Stone to be careful. 'I must stipulate that the handcuffs stay on for the entire time that you're outside these walls.'

'Yes, sir, of course.'

'I trust her passing will be pain free.'

Meak took a step back from the desk, his chains clanking, and offered a thin smile. 'Ma will be grateful, I'm sure.'

CHAPTER 1

TO EXACT REVENGE

Tuesday, 5 July

Rapid City's streets still wore the garlands of Independence Day celebrations. The oppressive heat seemed to ensnare the burnt powder of last night's firecrackers and the air was hazy and heavy.

Sam Ransom emerged from the post office with an armload of packages and envelopes fastened by string. His back was slightly bent but this was due to old age and hard living, not the weight of the family's mail he carried. The metal ferule of his hickory walking stick clacked on the wood as he limped across the boardwalk.

He stopped by the hitching rail where a palomino and a sorrel were tethered. His grey tailcoat over his linen shirt felt too heavy in this heat and he regretted his wife talking him into wearing it. He looked to his left and smiled. Charlotte, elegant as ever in her silver grey crinoline, strolled beside their daughter Jane. Both blonde women caught the eye of many male passers-by, and his chest swelled with pride.

Then his billfold twitched as he noticed that, between them, his women appeared to be carrying half the milliner's shop. In an attempt at quelling his ancestral meanness, he glanced to the right.

His son Adam was just about through loading the general stores into the back of the buckboard. The lad was fifteen, a year younger than his sister, and his physique was slight, small-boned, taking after his mother. Tall and wiry, Adam just didn't have the muscle to cope with loading so many crates. He'd better give the lad a hand, though the prospect of any physical activity in this heat was far from welcome.

He stepped down to the road and suddenly a whirlwind of dust and horseflesh engulfed him. The palomino's flank swayed hard against his side and thrust him headlong to the ground. His black Stetson flopped in the dust and the mail broke loose from its fastening and scattered on the hardpan.

Ransom gripped his stick tightly, turned on his side and glared upwards.

'Watch where you're going, old feller!' snapped the freshly mounted young blond man. The youth was in his early twenties, he guessed. Red checked shirt, leather vest and chaps. Small mean grey eyes set close together. Pistol butt out, resting on his hip. He appeared to be sober. Astride the sorrel, his slightly older companion wore a black moustache, which matched his shirt and jeans; he too was armed with a six-gun and carried a bullwhip.

'Sam!' Charlotte called, running over. 'Are you all right?'

As his wife reached his side, he took her offered hand

and eased himself to one knee. 'I'll live – no thanks to that young oaf, though!'

'Who're you calling an oaf, you stupid bastard?' the young man snarled, shifting his horse. His boot heel kicked at Ransom's shoulder.

Ransom tumbled from Charlotte's grasp and fell back in the dust.

'Easy, Wes,' growled the other rider.

Wes barked, 'Nobody calls me an oaf, Chad!'

Swiftly, Ransom snatched his old knife from its sheath beneath the tail of his coat and lunged under the palomino, ignoring the ache in his elderly limbs. He slashed at the cinch and rolled clear, suddenly breathless.

Wes yelled as he slid off his horse, still occupying his saddle. He landed noisily and harshly on his side. He was young and fit, however, and shuffled free and stood, his face livid and twisted in a snarl.

With the aid of his walking stick, Ransom heaved himself to his feet. He sheathed the knife and advanced on Wes. A pace away, he lashed out and the ferrule raised blood on the young man's cheek.

Suddenly, hands from behind thwarted further blows. Ransom's arms were gripped tight and he was pinned hard against the side of the sorrel. 'Nobody takes the stick to Wes Calhoun, Mister!' Chad said.

Laughing, Wes leapt forward and landed a punch to Ransom's jaw and another to his midriff. He tasted blood and felt sick. God, he was too old for this!

The train's whistle let out a plaintive wail as it approached the town.

Charlotte cried out, 'Stop it! Please stop!'

Ransom tried shrugging himself loose, his feet barely touching the ground, but the cowboy called Chad held him in a vice-like grip. His legs and knees felt weak and his heart pounded. He gasped for breath as each body blow from Wes punched the wind out of him. Fist after fist smashed into his face and he felt his lip split and tasted more blood.

Suddenly, the blows ceased. Through blurred eyes Ransom saw his daughter Jane bashing Wes Calhoun about the head with one of her purchases, while Adam's arms gripped the cowboy's raised arm and balled hand. 'Let my father be, you brute!' she sobbed.

'That's enough!' Chad shouted and abruptly let go of Ransom.

Sam Ransom's feet hit the dirt and his legs collapsed. The earth rose up to meet him and it hurt.

'Leave them!' Chad said.

'But, my saddle—'

'Pick it up tomorrow. Here, get on your horse before the law comes!'

He glimpsed vague shapes of the two horses as they wheeled round and headed out of town. Then he felt the firm grip of Charlotte's hand on his arm. 'Oh, Sam, what have you done?' she whispered. 'You're not setting a good example to the children.'

In spite of the pain that engulfed his body, he smiled.

'Seems to me he didn't have much choice in the matter, Ma,' Adam said as he approached, one eye swollen. He handed his father the black Stetson.

Charlotte ran up to her son and examined the lad's bruise. Then she turned and glared at Ransom. 'See what you've done now?'

He shook his head, and even that action hurt. 'Just help me up, will you, honey?' He used her arm for purchase and struggled to his feet. His insides felt all jumbled up and his stomach threatened to evict its contents. He fought that tendency and ran a hand over his aching chin and dabbed a fingertip on his lips: swollen and tender. 'That youth needs lessons in manners,' he mumbled, flicking his hat against indigo denim pants and setting up a small dust cloud.

Charlotte coughed and put a handkerchief to her mouth and nose. 'Maybe so, but it needs a younger man to do it,' she said in a muffled tone.

He put his hat on while Jane and Adam quickly collected the fallen mail.

'Sheriff's on his way over,' Adam said, handing his father the envelopes and a few small packages.

'Good. Maybe he can tell us a bit about Wes Calhoun and his pal Chad.' He stopped, his eye caught by the topmost package. He recognized the writing – Abner Nolan's spidery hand. Curious, he slid a finger under the flap and slit it open. Inside was a thin exercise book, completely filled with scrawled words, and a brief note. 'Maybe you could see about getting these poems published, old friend,' Abner wrote.

'Spot of trouble, Sam?' asked Sheriff Webb.

Ransom replaced the book and letter and looked up. 'Yes, Skip, I'd like to charge a young whelp by the name of Wes Calhoun. He kinda forgot his manners. Maybe you could find them for him in one of your cells sometime soon?'

Sheriff Skip Webb's face clouded and he took off his hat, scratched his straw-coloured hair. 'That won't be so easy. You know, his pa Jackson Calhoun owns the biggest spread round these parts and a fair portion of the town as well. Chad Burton's the outfit's ramrod.'

'Oh, it's that Calhoun. Figures,' Ransom said, not in the least surprised. Times hadn't changed all that much, it seemed, since he was the sheriff's age. Resignedly, he turned to his family. 'Let's be getting home.' He dumped the mail in the back of the wagon and added ruefully, 'I've got letters – and a handful of birthday cards – to read.' Next week was his sixty-second birthday and it looked like he'd be nursing a bruised body and ego instead of celebrating. Still, today, even with his massive aches, he was glad to be alive.

'Grateful?' snapped Matilda Meak from the bed she knew she'd never leave. 'Why should I be grateful? I'm dying, for God's sake! What have I got to be grateful about?'

'I'm just saying what Warden Trent said, Ma!'

'Don't you answer back like that, Justus!'

'Ma, don't go on so.' Gideon resembled his brother in many ways, though his dark brown hair was cut short and his eyes were the colour of shadow – umber. His thin pallid lips and receding chin were inherited from her late husband, God rest his damnable soul. 'He was only saying—'

'Now you both gang up against your poor mother, do you?' She scowled and eyed their handcuffs. 'What a sorry pair you've become. I only wish your poor father was here!'

'Shucks, we know, Ma,' said Gideon.

She let out a harsh laugh. 'Know? You know *nothing*!'

Justus moved nearer and sat on the side of her bed. He reached out a hand for hers, but she pulled away. 'Ma, we remember what you told us, about Pa being murdered an' all.'

'That wasn't the half of it, son,' she whispered bitterly.

Leaning closer, Justus said, 'What d'you mean, Ma?'

'Where's that lawmen you brung with you?' she whispered.

'Out on the porch rolling a smoke,' Gideon said softly.

13

He moved to the other side of the bed. 'Why're we whispering?'

'I don't want that lowdown skunk of a lawman to listen in, that's why.'

'I'll go check.' Gideon moved to the door, cracked it open a little. He nodded, pushed the door to and silently returned to her bedside. 'He's dozing in the rocker.'

'My chair,' she said in a raised tone then caught herself. She looked around at the poorly furnished room and her heart lurched when she glimpsed her reflection in the dressing table mirror. Her once auburn hair was now grey and thin, while her hazel eyes seemed dull, as if diluted pigment. Her thin lips pursed. The family nose was prominent, however, and both her sons took after her there. She tore her eyes away as flames of anger and frustration burned afresh in her breast. Now she must tell her boys and set them on their road of vengeance. 'There were six men in your father's gang,' she said, clearing her throat. She closed her eyes and recited, 'Carter, Ransom, Tylor, Baines and Nolan.'

'That's five,' Justus said.

Her eyes sprang open and impaled him. 'Your pa made up the six, idiot!'

'Oh, right.'

'What happened?' asked Gideon.

Her lower lip trembled. 'They decided to share their loot between five, that's what, and so your pa was shot in the back.' Tears blurred her vision. She glanced down at her hands, thin and worn like an old woman's and here she was only fifty-five. Going before her time. 'Those no-goods not only killed your pa, they ruined my life and yours as well.'

'We know that, Ma,' said Gideon. 'You've said it often enough, we could've ridden a straighter trail if we'd had Pa to guide us.'

'Well, it bears retelling.'

'Sure, Ma.'

Justus said, 'This is the first time you told us their names – the killers' names.'

'Well, I tried to bring you up right, but you still went down a crooked path. I didn't want you going out after them, claiming justice – though the Lord knows, your pa deserves it!'

'So why are you telling us now?' Gideon asked.

'Yeah, after all these years. We were about six when Pa was killed, right, Gideon?'

'So Ma says.'

'I had to bring you up, fend for you and feed and clothe you.'

'We know, and we're grateful—'

'Grateful! There's that word again.'

'You still haven't answered my question,' Gideon said. 'Why tell us now?'

She nodded and glanced down at her trembling thin hands. 'My conscience, I suppose. They left your pa for dead but he managed to get home and told me everything, how he'd been double-crossed and dry-gulched. They ran off with his share of the loot. A lot of money, it was. Money that should've been ours – now it could be yours.' She wiped tears away with the heel of her hand. 'I nursed him till he died.'

'But why now, Ma?' Gideon persisted.

She raised her head and eyed her sons. 'Because now you're men and you'll soon be free – free to exact revenge.'

'We still have four years left to serve,' said Gideon.

'Maybe two, if we get parole,' added Justus.

'Is that so? Well, the doctor tells me I have maybe two

weeks left to serve in this life, so I needed to speak to you both before my time was up.' Her hands reached out to each side, fingers interlacing with theirs. 'Don't fail me, boys. Do it for your father.'

Gideon looked across his mother at Justus.

She watched them, warm contentment in her chest, and smiled as Gideon said, 'We've got to get rid of Deputy Stone.'

Justus pursed his lips then nodded.

Gideon was the strong one, she knew. He'd do her bidding. And Justus, the weaker one, would follow.

She let go of their hands and twisted her thin right arm behind her, under the pillow and pulled out a Colt Model P .45. She was surprised how heavy it felt; when she'd put it there, its weight had barely signified. 'I thought you might need this,' she said. 'It's loaded.'

Blood drained from Justus's face.

Gideon nodded then took the weapon, hefted it, his handcuffs chinking.

As Gideon moved towards the door, she wanted to call to him, but that might alert the deputy. She'd dearly love to watch blood being spilled but consoled herself that she'd listen instead.

Gideon eased the door wide. Careful though he was, it creaked on rusted hinges. Hens ran free over the dusty ground, while a cock crowed. Deputy Stone's slumber seemed slightly disturbed by the sound, but he remained asleep, the half-smoked quirly dangling from his lips, a trail of ash on his leather vest, next to the tin star.

'I ain't staining Ma's chair, Deputy,' Gideon whispered and shoved the six-gun in his belt. He strode through the doorway, grabbed Stone's shirt collar and flung him from the rocker chair, off the porch onto the ground. Dust swirled as Stone woke, his face reflecting confusion.

'Sorry, but your job's done,' said Gideon and pulled out the pistol.

Stone's reflexes were fast. Sprawled and disoriented as he was, he still drew his Army Colt. But he was at an immense disadvantage. Before he could register on Gideon standing on the porch that he'd so recently occupied, two bullets thudded into his head. His trigger finger twitched and a single shot churned up dust.

Half-turning, Gideon called through the doorway, 'I guess we're free, brother.'

Their mother let out a mirthless cackle. 'Free to hunt down those murdering swine at last!'

CHAPTER 2

YOUNG GUNS

'This is the last of the stores,' said Adam as he hauled a big crate labelled 'Fine china'.

'Go easy with that, son. That's my surprise for your mother.'

Adam grinned, and his bruised eyelid flinched at the action. 'Not much of a surprise, Pa – it has a label on it!'

'Yes, well, I had my arm twisted. This was the perfect gift for her, so she said.'

'Sometimes, Pa, I wonder if I'll ever get wed.'

'Why's that?'

'I reckon I have a mind of my own – I don't want it changed by a woman.'

Despite the aches of his old bones and the damage inflicted by Wes Calhoun, Ransom laughed. It hurt, but it did him some good.

Later, his belly full, he lowered himself to the porch bench seat with Charlotte. He smoked a cigar and was content. From here they'd often watch the sun set and the stars fill the sky. Sunset was a good two hours off yet. 'That was a fine meal, honey,' he said, patting his paunch. 'For chicken, it was a mite spicy – what was that flavour?'

'Tang gave me the recipe. It's called Chicken *diablo*. What you tasted was the mustard and curry.'

'He's a wonder, that Tang. The hands really enjoy his concoctions!'

'I must admit I was a little surprised that you kept anything down after the beating you took.'

He sighed. 'I've had worse.'

'I know, but you were younger then,' she said. 'A lot younger.'

'Don't remind me.' He grimaced. 'Every time you do that, I reckon I get a year older.'

She hugged him and he winced as his ribs rebelled. 'That hurts,' he whispered.

'Love hurts, Sam. I want us to grow old together but we can't do that if you pick fights with young troublemakers.'

'*I* didn't pick the fight.'

She eyed the walking stick resting against the wall by his side.

He noticed there was still a fleck or two of blood on the ferrule. He smiled at the recollection and picked it up. 'Let's take a walk round our homestead,' he said.

'I'd like that. We haven't done so in quite a while.'

'Nope, we haven't. We should do it more often. Shows us how fortunate we've been.' He looked down at her as they stepped off the porch. 'I was lucky to find you, Charly.'

'You haven't called me that in a while either.'

'No?' He kissed her and ignored the pain in his lip. Their touch lingered. When he broke the moment and stepped back, he said, 'I think it all the time. My Charly.'

'Those were wild days, Sam.' Gently, her hand brushed his bruised jaw and her features clouded. 'Maybe best forgotten.'

He shook his head and he felt sure some bits were still loose inside his skull. 'Not by me, Charly.'

They strolled slowly to accommodate his limp. They passed the well at the side of the steps leading up to the porch. A hardened surface led away to the ranch entrance, the large shingle swaying in the evening breeze. Beyond was an avenue of pine trees. Ahead, on the northern side of the ranch enclosure stood the bunkhouse and cookhouse, where lights glowed. 'The men will be enjoying Tang's chow mein tonight,' she said.

'I'm sure they're getting fat and idle, you know,' he said.

She nudged his arm with a fist. 'Don't be silly. They work really hard for you, and you know it!'

By now his back felt clammy with sweat. It was an infernally hot evening. They passed the pile of logs against the side of the single-storey ranch house, then a series of bushes that concealed the outhouse from the main building. Crickets made a raucous sound as they approached the back of the house, where tilled rows of vegetables and herbs shimmered in the breeze. He knew how proud Charly was of her kitchen garden.

He suddenly winced and stopped walking, insistent pain stabbing up his leg.

'Are you all right, Sam? Do you want to go in?' She gestured toward the back door.

'No, I'm fine. I'd expect this in the winter, but not in this heat.' He wiped a sleeve across his forehead. 'Old age, I guess.' He moved on again, past the sad selection of small wooden crosses that signified the family's pet cemetery. Over in the southeast corner of the enclosure was a collection of bur oak saplings, their leaves rustling. He paused at the water pump and ladled a mouthful from the bucket. It tasted quite refreshing, but lacked any kind of bite.

'You want a brandy when we get in?' she asked, reading his mind, hand pressing his arm.

'Sounds like a good idea.' He swung his stick in the direction of the stables and corral on the southern side. 'Let's check on the horses, first.'

The barn was large, a two-storey building, with ample space for the buckboard and stalls for six horses. Charly's palomino, Jack, was slightly skittish as they entered, while the others stood quite docile. A touch and a word from her and all was calm.

Sam ran a hand down the flank of his buckskin, Bodie, and the flesh shivered to his touch. 'Good fella,' he whispered, 'I see Hank's been taking real good care of you. Maybe you and me will take a ride tomorrow, eh?'

The horse snorted and nodded its head.

'I swear that horse understands every word you say!' Charly said and laughed.

'Of course he does!'

When they shut the barn door behind them and headed for the porch steps, she asked, 'Where are you thinking of going tomorrow?'

'Nowhere special.' He used the stick to point at the rolling foothills now bathed in the mauve shades of the coming night. 'I'll probably just sit astride Bodie and admire the land we've acquired over the years.'

'Hard years, Sam.' She brushed up close to him, head against his arm. 'Especially when you weren't here.'

As his hand brushed her hair, it held a slight tremor – guilt over his absence, or another sign of old age, or a hangover from the beating he'd taken? 'You coped, even with two kids,' he said. 'I knew you would.' He'd missed so much, often risking his life for complete strangers. He'd been a driven man, then. Now, he just felt worn out.

As they climbed the steps to the porch, he gazed at the stars, and then at Charly's love-filled eyes, and he felt that he was the luckiest man alive.

Starlight glimmered above the small backwater town but Justus and Gideon had no eyes for the sky. The brothers stepped through the batwings and surveyed the men gathered then strode up to the bar. The saloon was full and smoke filled the air.

Dave, the barkeep, smiled in recognition and put their preferred liquor bottle and two glasses in front of them. 'I've got some news for you guys, if you're interested.'

'Sure, Dave.' Gideon flipped a dollar and Dave caught it. 'Keep the change.'

'Cheers.' He pocketed the coin and nodded to the far corner. A game of faro was in progress, six cowpokes lounging in chairs around the table. 'Two cowboys – the tow-headed one and the gangly guy.'

'Right, thanks. Gimme two more glasses.' Dave nodded and complied. Gideon grabbed the bottle and Justus picked up the glasses. 'Let's go recruiting, brother.'

It was obvious that the two cowboys were down on their luck and not faring well at the table. Gideon leaned between them and whispered, 'If you two gentlemen want to step over to our table, my brother and I have a proposition you might find worthwhile.'

'Worthwhile as in money?' asked the tow-headed one; he was as big as an ox.

'That's right,' said Justus.

The two cowboys exchanged looks and simultaneously threw in their cards and shoved back their chairs. 'Sorry, folks, we've got business to attend to,' said the tow-headed one, retrieving his high-crowned Mexican hat from the chair back. 'Thanks for the game.'

'Yeah, pleasure's all ours,' said the dealer, eyeing the money pot in the centre of the table.

Once seated in a shadowy corner, Gideon poured a generous measure into each glass. 'I'm Gideon Meak and this is my brother Justus,' he said.

'Turner Kimball.' He was about twenty, Gideon reckoned. He possessed a gourdlike nose, a doughy complexion and lignite eyes.

The gangly one had straw-coloured hair. He seemed about four or five years older than Kimball. 'Name's Quincy Newton. Barkeep said you were looking for help to dig up a fortune of money.' His sandy eyes glinted, as if shards of gold hid in them. He brushed a dirty finger against his bulbous nose and squinted. 'So, what do you want us to do?'

Gideon's thin pallid lips smiled. 'We need to find a bunch of back-shooters and when we do we'll also get more money than we've ever seen in our lives. Equal shares.'

Kimball grinned. 'Sounds good to me.'

'Count me in,' said Newton.

Wednesday, 6 July

'Count that again, Mr Ingal,' snapped the muscular young man, leaning over the general store counter, where a scattering of coins amounted to less than five dollars. He slammed a fist down and his purchases, a half dozen stogies, jumped as if in fright. 'You short-changed me!'

'No, Mr Ashby, I assure you I didn't,' the store owner said. With a shaky finger he slid his spectacles up to the bridge of his nose and glanced at the four male customers for support. Gideon and the others watched, faces impassive. Ashby was in his early twenties, Gideon reckoned, but he'd lived hard: askew broken nose and a lengthy scar on his right cheek testified to that. He wore his tawny hair long under a black derby hat with an eagle feather in its band.

'Everyone will tell you,' Ingal said, 'I'm most punctilious about—'

'You calling me a liar?'

Ingal backed away, raising his hands slightly. 'No, sir. But I know what I know!'

'I've a good mind to climb over this counter and whup you, damnit!'

Suddenly, Ingal reached under the counter and raised his twelve-bore shotgun and levelled it on Ashby. 'I've had it with you, Ashby. Stop riling me! I ain't selling to McMasters and that's final!'

'Hey, steady with that thing, it's liable to go off,' said Ashby, taking a step back from the counter. 'Anyway, what do you mean, "sell"? What're you talking about?'

'I know the game McMasters plays. He built his empire on threats and coercion! I'm telling you to leave or I'll plug you!'

'Yeah, OK,' said Ashby and for a second Ingal visibly relaxed. Ashby's Colt 1877 Lightning lived up to its name, his right hand a sudden blur as he drew and fired.

Ingal stared, aghast, dropped his shotgun and lurched backwards against the shelving. The single bullet hole centred over his heart. He was dead before he hit the floorboards.

'Nobody calls me a liar.' Ashby turned to the four witnesses and blithely holstered his gun. His misty blue eyes were cold as he scratched a Lucifer on the counter top and lit up a stogie.

At that instant, the sheriff entered the store. 'Give up your weapon, Ashby!' he barked, his own six-gun drawn.

Ashby gestured with his cigar at the four witnesses. 'Did you see that?'

'Sure did,' Gideon Meak said. 'It was self-defence.' He turned to the others. 'Isn't that so?'

'Yeah,' said Justus. Newton and Kimball nodded.

'Fair fight, Sheriff, seems to me,' Gideon said.

The sheriff shook his head and holstered his gun. 'Maybe.' He glared at Ashby. 'I want you out of this town by nightfall, Ashby. I've had enough of your "fair fights" in my town. Is that clear?'

Ashby shrugged. 'It don't seem right or fair to me, Sheriff, but as it is I'm hankering after fresh pastures.' He smiled.

The sheriff let out an angry growl. 'I'll send the undertaker over.' He turned on his heel and left.

'Thanks for the support back there,' Ashby said.

'Glad to help,' Gideon replied. 'Seems to me, Ashby, we could use a man with your talent.'

'Is that so?'

'Yes, we're on a recruiting drive. We need young guns. Fast guns like you.'

Ashby grinned. 'Well, once I've got my payment off of Mr McMasters, I'll be a free agent again. Tell me more.'

Thursday, 7 July

The five gunmen rode out of the livery mid-morning but didn't get far before someone shouted from across the street: 'Is one of you Gideon Meak?'

Gideon reined in his horse and looked at the speaker on

the opposite boardwalk. He was a willowy young man in a fawn calico shirt and jeans with a low-crowned flat-brimmed hat.

'Who wants to know?' Gideon said.

'Irvin Hardee,' he said. 'I've heard you've been asking around.'

'So?'

'So I've got good information – if you'll cut me in.'

Gideon urged his horse across the street and stopped in front of Irvin. The willowy youth had midnight-blue eyes, coal-black hair, a pencil-line moustache and flaring nostrils. He looked very young, untried by life, save for three deep scars down the left side of his face.

'How old are you, Hardee?'

'Nineteen.' He hesitated, hitched his hands on his gun-belt; he carried a Navy Colt. 'I've been around – escaped prison, as it happens.'

'That may be a recommendation, I guess. What have you got to tell me?'

'I want to join you.'

'OK. The amount we're talking, one more share won't matter all that much.'

Irvin grinned. 'I'll go get my horse.'

'What about the information?'

'When I'm riding with you, I'll tell you.'

For a young gun, Gideon mused, he was wary and wily.

Later, on the trail, Irvin told them. 'There's a drunk in Sturgis. Believe it or not, he's a barber. The word is, don't get a shave in the morning, he's liable to shake a bit. . . .'

'You're sure?' Gideon demanded.

'Yeah. His name's Jubal Baines.'

Gideon and Justus exchanged glances and smiled. *At last!*

Irvin added, 'And when he's in the saloon he never stops

talking about the old days when he was a young gun.' He laughed. 'Old fool!'

CHAPTER 3

BADLY KNITTED BONES

Sunday, 8 May, 1859

'My pa is very interested in your mine, Mr Ransom,' Willis Hearst said as the pair of them clambered down the incline of the Comstock mineshaft.

'That gladdens my heart, Mr Hearst,' Ransom said. 'My partners will be pleased to hear that, too.'

'There's four of you in the partnership, is that right?' Ransom reckoned Hearst was about four or five years younger than him, yet young Hearst had a confident bearing, probably inherited from his father, Wayne, who didn't suffer fools gladly.

'Yes. Rory, me and Abner started mining here, then we got some help from Brax and made him a partner.'

'Brax?'

'Braxton's known as the "dandy miner" – hails from Charleston and can charm the ears off any woman. But he's a good worker.'

'I see. Well, my offer will have to be split four ways – will your partners be happy with that?'

Ransom nodded. 'We've sunk a lot of labour, time and money into it and just want a fair return.'

'That you'll get,' Hearst said.

Kerosene lamps hung from upright beams at regular intervals; Brax had refilled them not half an hour earlier. Their shadows danced on the walls of barren rock. Moisture glinted on belts of partly decomposed porphyry and sheets of clay. Running parallel with the incline of the shaft was a wide vein of ore.

'We regularly bring up two or three tons a week,' Ransom said.

'I heard.'

Ransom smiled. Hearst and his father doubtless knew that the silver ore fetched about $3,000 a ton. Transport and smelting would eat into that, but there was still plenty of profit left over. Ransom and his three partners were rich already. Selling off the mine was simply the icing on the cake.

Hearst glanced warily at the timber supports, which seemed to bow under the weight of earth. 'I'm not too happy about the geology of Nevada, particularly this place,' he added.

'Post-and-cap timbering works in mines,' Ransom argued.

Hearst stepped in a puddle and swore. 'Yes but, like many miners, you've encountered underground reservoirs.'

'It's one way to get a hot bath,' Ransom joked.

'Maybe so. Maybe the hot water can be used in time. But for now it makes the lode unstable.'

Ransom stopped in a section with wooden beams on

either side and above, like a doorway, and hunkered down to ease the ache in his neck from constant crouching while he walked. 'Are you looking for ways to drop your offer – or maybe reduce it?'

Apparently not averse to getting his clothes muddy, Hearst lowered to one knee beside Ransom. 'No, I stand by my father's word. I've a mind to call in a friend, that's all. A consultant from Germany. He may come up with an alternative to the post-and-cap method of timbering.'

Ransom grinned. 'So you'll go ahead and purchase our mine?'

'I will recommend my father goes ahead, yes.'

'That's great. Wait till I tell my partners! They'll be—'

Suddenly, a short distance ahead of them, a brief, loud explosion sounded. The walls of the shaft seemed to shift and waver, as if fluid.

Ransom growled, 'Look out!' And he thrust himself at Hearst, pushing the man backwards, away from him, back up the slope. Seconds later, amidst dust and flying rubble and mud, the wooden beams crashed down on Ransom's legs with tremendous force. He blacked out with the pain.

Thursday, 7 July, 1892

Ransom dismounted and left Bodie to graze. Wheezing, he limped up the slight slope and tried to ignore the burning sensation over his ribs at each breath.

He topped the rise and surveyed the land spread out before him – his land, the Ransom land.

Grazing beef dotted the meadows. About a mile away, the ranch house in its fenced enclosure. Mere silhouettes, Hank and two fresh stallions he was breaking in.

He lowered himself to a large boulder and rested his troublesome leg. He was sorely reminded of those far-off days.

At times, the cold winters were terrible: the piercing signal from his badly knitted bones brought to mind again the whole sorry mess of over thirty years ago.

Sunday, 8 May, 1859

Ransom's leg had been broken in two places. But his prompt action saved Hearst from a similar or worse fate.

About an hour later, writhing in agony, Ransom regained his senses in the medical tent. He learned that while he'd lain unconscious, Hearst had hurried up the shaft's slope and got help. Even though he must have feared a further cave in, Hearst returned with two men and a couple of wood boards. They'd tied Ransom to these and hauled him up and out.

Laudanum stilled most of his pain, but it didn't help his hearing. Every sound from outside seemed damped down, as if he was listening to it through layers of cloth. He shook his head, and the memory persisted. The crashing noise he'd heard hadn't been a cave-in and landfall. No, it had definitely been an explosion further down the shaft. A chilly sensation trailed his spine as he realized what had happened. If they hadn't paused to chinwag, they'd both have been killed. But who'd want to sabotage the mine? Maybe young Hearst had enemies and the mine was a means to an end?

Fighting the intermittent waves of pain as he lay there, Ransom kept looking anxiously at the entrance flap for any sign of Mattie Dryden, the saloon girl who'd won his heart.

But she never appeared. When two of his partners visited him, he asked them about her whereabouts.

Rory looked sheepish, glanced at Abner, then back at him, and finally said, 'We heard that she packed her bags and left, not long after you went down the mine with Mr Hearst.'

Ransom studied the pair. Abner's eyes evaded his and he suddenly seemed to find his shoes of great interest.

'What are you not telling me?' Ransom demanded.

'You'd better tell him,' mumbled Abner.

Rory nodded, cleared his throat and blurted out, 'She ran off with Brax.'

'Brax?' That had hurt a lot, even more than the broken bones.

Then, a couple of days later, Rory discovered that when Braxton left, he cleaned out their bank account in its entirety. Only then did the realization hit Ransom. Brax had been in the mineshaft earlier; he must have lit the fuse for the explosive to go off.

'Go find him,' Ransom said between gritted teeth. 'If I could, you know I'd come with you.'

'We'll try, Sam,' Rory said. 'You just get set on making a full recovery.'

He recovered all right, though he was then saddled with a permanent limp. But he was determined it wouldn't affect his life. One evening, while he used a crutch to get around the mining camp, he was accosted by a voice out of the darkness between two tents.

'Mr Ransom, might I have a word?'

He stopped and steadied himself. It was easier to keep moving than balance on one leg and a crutch. He had no intention of relying on any damned crutch for the rest of his life, so he hoped he'd get the hang of it after a while.

'Yes, who is it?'

A tall plump man stepped into the light of what served as the main street. 'I'm Wayne Hearst.' He held out a hand. 'I'd like to thank you for saving my son. He told me what you did – and at what cost to yourself.'

Ransom gripped the old man's hand. A firm honest handshake. 'Glad I was able to save him, Mr Hearst.'

'Now don't take this the wrong way, but I heard about your crook of a partner and I'd like to offer you a pecuniary reward for your services to my family.'

Shaking his head, Ransom smiled. 'Sorry, sir, but I'm no bounty hunter and I don't do things to get any reward, save maybe at Judgement Day from my Maker.'

'But—'

'That's my final word on the subject, Mr Hearst.' Ransom offered his hand.

'Well, all right,' said Hearst, shaking hands again. 'But if you ever need help in any way whatsoever, call on me, Mr Ransom. I owe you – and I always pay my debts.'

'Thanks, sir. I'll bear that in mind.' He turned away and limped further up the main street.

His two friends returned four weeks later, but they hadn't located Braxton.

Ransom felt sure that their paths would cross again.

CHAPTER 4

BUR OAK SPRINGS

Friday, 8 July

Luckily for the men of Sturgis, the 14-year-old town boasted two barber shops. As the two Meak brothers strode under the shingle, Jubal Baines, Haircuts and Shaves, Gideon surmised that most folk frequented the other one, since Jubal's was without any customers. He and Justus opened the door, walked in and hung their hats on the pegs by the entrance.

'What'll it be, gents?' asked the stoop-shouldered old man at the scabrous leather chair.

'Jubal, is it?' asked Gideon.

'That's my name over the door.' He was tall and thin, his hair white. He had long sideburns and a moustache. His bulbous nose was red and veined. Gideon glimpsed checked wool pants and a blue linen shirt under the barber's big stained apron.

'A shave and a trim,' said Gideon.

'Me, I don't want a cut – just a shave,' said Justus, a hand rasping his whiskers.

'Sure.' Baines reached for a shaving brush and a cup and stirred up foaming soap. 'A good lather is half a good shave,' he opined. 'Now, who'd like to be first?' He grinned and revealed crooked teeth.

Gideon stepped forward and settled into the seat while Justus found a chair by the window.

Hands shaking slightly, Baines draped the white linen coverlet over Gideon and tied it at the back of his neck. 'What was it you wanted, again?'

Gideon noticed a deep dent in the barber's forehead and eyed the barber's trembling fingers. He decided to forego the shave. 'Just a trim.'

'Right.' Appearing slightly flustered, Baines moved aside the cup and shaving brush on the counter under the mirror and finally located a pair of scissors.

'You're new around here,' Baines said as he snipped.

'Yes, just passing through. Looking for someone.'

'Hey, you're not bounty hunters, are you?'

'No. We're after an old friend.'

Baines chuckled. 'I came across a few bounty hunters in my time, you know.'

'Is that so?'

'Yep. Used to be a deputy sheriff – we're going way back now, of course. Can't hardly recall the details.' He tapped his forehead with the scissors. 'Memory's not what it was, you know.'

'Is that so?'

'Didn't you just say that?'

Gideon laughed. 'Seems there's nothing wrong with your memory, Mister.'

Baines shrugged and cut off a large clump of hair. 'Oops, sorry... I'll put that right so's nobody'll notice.'

'Yes, you do that.'

'What's your friend's name? Maybe I know him – or her.'

'There's a few of them, old timer. Ransom, Carter, Tyler and Nolan.'

The scissors stopped. 'Hey, that's a coincidence, I used to work with those guys!'

'Is that so?'

The shop door rattled as Justus shut it and turned the 'Open' sign to face inwards.

Baines craned his neck round and demanded, 'Hey, Mister, why've you shut my shop? It's early yet.'

Under the coverlet, Gideon cocked his Colt. 'Let's you and us go upstairs to your rooms, shall we?'

Baines gulped. 'I don't have much money, Mister.'

Gideon flung off the coverlet and pressed the barrel of the revolver against the barber's side. 'We're after information, not your money.'

'Oh, right. . . .'

With Baines leading the way, they climbed the back stairs to the landing. Off here were two doors. Baines turned the handle of the one on the left. 'This is my room, but you won't find money—'

Gideon shoved Baines inside and the barber sprawled on the bare boards. 'Your memory sure is going, old timer! We want information about your old pals.'

'But I don't recollect—'

Gideon lunged forward and smashed the barrel of his revolver across the barber's face, splitting his cheek. 'Start using that memory!' He holstered his gun and turned to his brother. 'Search the place.'

Justus shut the door after them and went round the small room, ransacking the drawers and wardrobe, disturbing the small amount of clothing. 'This looks interesting,' he said, opening a drawer that contained a bunch of letters, citations and other documents.

'Hey,' Baines exclaimed, 'they're my keepsakes – when I was a deputy. . . .'

Justus laughed. 'You, a deputy? What a laugh!'

'I can recall that—'

Gideon punched Baines. 'You'll recall what I want you to! Now tell me where we can find Ransom and the others!'

A trembling hand covering his bleeding face, Baines peered up at his persecutor. 'Honest to God, Mister, I don't remember. . . .'

Unsheathing his knife, Gideon said, 'You will, old timer, I'll make sure you will.'

Saturday, 9 July

From the same boulder, Ransom surveyed his ranch and land yet again.

He took a small swig from the flask of brandy Charly had slipped into his jacket earlier. Thoughtful, considerate and loving. What had he done to deserve her? Best not to question his continued good luck, he thought.

He was mending slowly and could walk a fair distance now without wheezing, without his ribs burning and aching.

July, 1866

Twenty-six years ago, he'd been aching too. Saddle-sore and annoyed, he and his four deputies had been on the trail of a stagecoach for two blistering hot days.

His trusted deputies were Abner and Rory and two men who'd joined up with them in the War Between the States:

Jubal and Darby. Good friends, and good with a gun, all of them. As they fought side by side, Ransom thought it seemed mighty ironic that the gold from the Comstock Lode helped finance the Union – against Braxton's side, the Confederacy. But that conflict was already a year old. Strange, he should think of Brax now.

According to the coach-line's manager, there were four passengers onboard – and a secret consignment of $30,000. 'Not as secret as you hoped, then, was it?' Ransom said.

'That has us worried, yes,' the manager said. 'They left the shotgun rider dead, but they've still got our driver, Toothy Watson.'

'Any idea why they took the coach?'

The manager shrugged. 'Probably didn't have the means to transfer the bullion. Or perhaps they wanted the passengers as hostages. I'm only guessing.'

'Would your company pay for their release?'

He shook his head. 'I've been instructed to refuse any demands of ransom . . . er, Mr Ransom.'

Rory stepped forward. 'They might use the passengers as shields instead.'

Ransom nodded. 'When we catch up with the bastards, doubtless we'll get to put your theory to the test.'

And now they were close. Very close.

Mountains loomed, about ten miles northeast.

Tracks of six horses accompanied the stagecoach, four of them carrying riders; they probably had a couple of men driving the coach. So the odds were about even, Ransom reckoned.

Abner was the best tracker and scouted the trail ahead, while Ransom, Rory, Darby and Jubal followed; all spread out and walked their horses at a slow pace to limit the amount of telltale dust.

It was two hours after noon when Abner rode back to join them. 'There's a narrow gorge that cuts into the mountain, about two miles ahead. If it's the place I reckon it is, they've boxed themselves in.'

'Or they're setting an ambush,' suggested Darby.

'Yes,' Abner conceded, 'that's possible.'

'Let's take extra care, then,' Ransom said. 'We may be the only hope those passengers have.'

When Ransom and Abner climbed up the old goat trail to the bluff above the far end of Narrow Gorge, Ransom was surprised to find no lookout posted. He whispered over his shoulder, 'I guess they aren't planning an ambush.'

Abner shrugged. 'Maybe they'll send someone up later, before dark sets in.'

'Maybe.' Cautiously, Ransom crawled to the edge and let out a gasp. 'Well, I'll be damned.'

'What is it?'

'Take a look – but keep out of sight.'

Abner shuffled forward and stopped by his side. It was a spectacular view. Ahead was a massive natural rock basin in the mountain, and the only entry appeared to be through the gorge. The bowl was oval in shape, running in a southeast direction. The steep sides were clad with fir trees on the northeast slopes and bur oak on the southwest. Below the oak trees was a large pond, its water clearly polluted by the rotting carcasses of two mountain goats. On the left of the pond was an old water tower.

In the centre of the bowl was a small town, not much more than a main street and a collection of wooden buildings, perhaps twenty of them, all in a derelict state. A cemetery was halfway up the eastern side of the basin, while among the trees on the eastern slopes were four black pits.

'I reckon they're the mine entrances,' Abner said.

'You know this place? It looks deserted.'

'It is. Yep, I remember it now. It was a gold-mining boom-town, fed from an underwater spring. They dug a lot of money out of those holes, till things went wrong for them.'

'What happened?'

'Winters were bad in the mountains, anyway, but here it was worse. Flooding swamped the south side of town.' Abner pointed. 'See, some of them were rebuilt on stilts?'

Ransom nodded. 'Why didn't they just move to the other side of the basin – where it didn't flood?'

'Some folk did. But come next summer, the water spring dried up – and so did the gold.'

'They just up and left, same as in so many gold-mine towns, I guess.'

'Yep.' Abner swept his arm to encompass the entire basin. 'There's nothing here to keep a man and his family. Only the gold drew them.'

Ransom spotted movement at the far end of the town and grabbed Abner's arm. 'Get down!' he snapped.

The pair hunkered behind a big out-jutting rock, just the tops of their heads showing above. Ransom pointed.

Livery stable doors swung open briefly and Ransom glimpsed the stagecoach inside. 'I wonder where they're keeping the hostages.'

The moon was full when Ransom indicated the goat trail that led down the southern slope into the basin. Darby nodded and Ransom went first. After descending about forty feet, he encountered trees and waved for the others to follow. Below his silhouette, the trees cast black shadows.

The rest went down, save for Abner who remained on the lip of the bowl, his Spencer .56-.56 loaded and ready. He was a crack shot, with a marksman's superb eyesight.

They negotiated their way through the bur oaks and emerged from the trees at the edge of the stagnant pond. Ransom was sweating and wondered if the wood tower on the left held decent water; doubtful. Another hot night. He signed for Darby and Jubal to move to the left – west of the town – while he and Rory would move to the east.

Their plan was simple enough. 'First light, we go in,' Ransom said. 'Then we search the buildings from one end of the town to the other till we locate the hostages.' While Ransom banked on them being in the livery stable, he couldn't take a chance on being wrong.

He and Rory moved to the rear of a derelict building, its purpose unknown, and sat on the ground with their backs against the wood wall. 'Now we wait,' Ransom whispered.

Dawn light touched the eastern lip of the natural basin and gradually lit the ridge all round. But sunlight would be a while creeping into the vast hollow. The western end – the basin entrance, Narrow Gorge, was lit first, the rock face shimmering.

Ransom and Rory stood to un-kink their muscles. Both withdrew their six-guns. Ransom peered through the building's broken glass window. Inside was filled with shadows, but he made out piles of old books on a bookshelf, their spines with scientific names.

Rory moved to the back step and the door opened to his touch. He swung it wide, and it was loose on its bottom hinge. Treading carefully, they crossed the dust-covered floor.

'Nobody's been in here for a long time,' Ransom whispered.

Then they passed through a doorway into a front office with a counter and scales, weights and shelving. The large office window was cracked in several places, and the legend painted across it read Dobson, Assays And Legal Claims in reverse lettering.

Outside, the dusty main street was pocked with sage-brush and clusters of weeds. Fresh wheel tracks cut into the dust, leading to the livery opposite.

Suddenly, Ransom heard shooting and sidled with his back to the wall; Rory followed his lead on the other side of the windowpane.

'I guess Darby and Jubal found some robbers,' Rory whis-pered.

Ransom nodded. 'Let's use it as a diversion.' He swung open the office front door, a hand hastily raised to stop the tinkling bell. Seconds later, he dashed across the street at an angle, Rory's pounding feet just behind him. He ran down the alley that cut between a derelict saloon – The Whiskey House – and Eidson's Livery.

A horse snickered inside. There was a loading loft above and Ransom gestured at it. Rory nodded in understanding and Ransom clambered up onto Rory's shoulders and leaped, fingers grabbing the edge of the opening. He hauled himself in, then ducked his head out and signed for Rory to wait.

Rory pulled out his Army Colt, ready.

Holding his breath, Ransom stepped inside, over the straw-covered wooden boards. Below, the stagecoach stood with its shafts still attached to four horses. He noticed a sprawled figure to one side of the front wheel. And tethered by her wrists to the back wheel was a kneeling blonde woman, her mouth covered by a cloth gag, the material obviously torn from the edge of her gingham dress.

He strained to listen for any voices or other signs of robbers, but he detected nothing. He crossed the loft and climbed down the ladder.

At sight of him, the woman's eyes widened in shock then she must have spotted Ransom's badge and she blinked, the startled look quickly fading. He hurried to her side and was assailed by her subtle perfume. He released the gag and she gasped for air.

'I'm Marshal Ransom,' he whispered, withdrawing his Bowie knife.

'Oh, thank God!' she said, her full lips an attractive soft flesh colour. Then, her tone grew sombre. 'But you can't fight all of them alone.' She let out a sob. 'That poor man tried,' she said and nodded at the corpse.

'Don't worry, I'm with four deputies.' He cut the rope bonds.

'Then you might have a chance.' She leaned against the side of the stagecoach, hands rubbing her wrists. He noticed she wasn't wearing a wedding band on her finger.

She started at the sound of tapping on the livery door.

'That's all right, Miss, it's one of my deputies. Rory.' Ransom ran to the Judas door and lifted the latch and let Rory in.

Returning to the dead man, Ransom knelt on one knee. He placed a hand on the man's shoulder and glanced up at her. 'There were supposed to be four passengers,' he said. 'Where are the other two?'

She regained her feet and pushed a stray curl of hair from her forehead. 'One of them was a gang member – calls himself Ollie Pascoe. The other was taken away with the driver, Mr Watson.'

'That makes it seven,' said Rory. 'Odds are lengthening.'

Ransom grunted in response and gently turned the dead man over. He swore under his breath.

'What's the matter?' Rory asked.

'I know him.' Blood drained from his face. 'It's Wayne Hearst.'

'From Comstock?'

'The same.' Ransom stood.

'It was awful,' she said. 'Even in the coach, the Pascoe man wore his black sombrero. Throughout the journey, he leered at me. When we were brought here, Pascoe threatened he'd have his way with me,' she said. 'Mr Hearst bravely stepped in to stop him – and got a bullet.' Her face crumpled and tears spilled. 'It was awful.'

'Then what happened?' Ransom demanded through gritted teeth.

'Their leader – Braxton, he was called – he—'

'*Braxton*?' Ransom echoed, his heart racing.

'Braxton? I don't believe this,' Rory said.

'Yes. Braxton.' She looked at both of them, her brow creased.

Somehow, Ransom regained control of his feelings, though they were in turmoil. 'Go on,' he grated.

'Well, Braxton told Pascoe to stop. They had the loot to take care of, he said.'

'Interesting.' Ransom rummaged in a compartment under the stagecoach seat. He pulled out a blanket and covered Wayne Hearst with it.

'What the hell are they doing here?' Rory asked.

Ransom shrugged. 'This might be a good place to hide the loot – till the heat wears off.'

Chuckling, Rory added, 'Though they don't know how close the heat is already, eh?'

'Could be.' He eyed the woman. 'Anything else you can tell us?'

She nodded. 'Not much. One of them has carrot-coloured hair, called Alvin Forrest. Another is tall and bald

– doesn't wear a hat; he's called Tim Burnside.'

'You're very observant, miss.'

'I was a journalist back East.'

'Figures. Anything else?'

'The only other name I caught was George Scott. He scowled a lot. He has a bushy black beard and he's a really big man, likely able to crush somebody with one hand.' She shuddered at the memory.

'Thanks. That information might prove useful.' He briefly rested a hand on her shoulder, and he felt a strange sensation assail his senses at the touch. 'You'd better stay here, Miss, till we find Braxton and the rest of the gang.'

'Don't worry, I'll do as you say. By the way, my name's Miss Charlotte Palmer,' she said, pale blue eyes openly appraising him. She held out her delicate-looking hand. 'Thank you for rescuing me, Marshal Ransom.'

Tempted to shake hands, instead he doffed his hat briefly. 'Pleasure's all mine, Miss Palmer.'

The date was etched into his memory, because it was the day he met Charlotte and fell in love at first sight: 21 July, 1866.

CHAPTER 5

URGENT MESSAGE

Sunday, 10 July, 1892

'I sure miss you, Ellie Rose,' Abner said. He stood over the solitary grave, black felt hat in one hand, a bunch of white pansies in the other, the Spencer .56-56 in the crook of his arm. Early morning sun scorched sparse tussocks of grass. 'I know it's been six months now, but your passing still burns my heart a mite too much.' A large flat rock served as a headstone:

Ellie Rose Nolan
Devoted Mother & Wife
6 June, 1852–5 January, 1892

On the left, wilting flowers stuck out of a tin can. To the right lay a small weathered wooden box.

With the aid of the Spencer rifle, Abner lowered himself to his knees at the graveside. He removed the sun-dried flowers and replaced them with the pansies. Then he fished in the pocket of his leather vest and withdrew a slip of paper. 'This here is my latest poem, Ellie Rose. Specially written for you.' He pulled out his wire-rimmed spectacles, put them on then from his vest pocket took a short pencil, licked its lead and marked three exes at the bottom of the sheet. He lifted the lid of the box, removed an earlier poem, pocketed it, and left the new one.

'You really should send some of them poems to the newspaper,' Ellie Rose told him more than once. 'They make my heart churn in a nice way.'

'No, honey, I write them just for you.' And now he found he couldn't seem to stop.

Out of sight, a couple of horses whickered in the direction of his homestead at the base of the hill and broke into his reverie. It was too early for Reverend Higgins to be calling, he reckoned. Sounded like they're coming up this way. He replaced the pencil in his pocket and made to move, but pain lanced into his joints.

Dadblamed knees have seized up. One more reminder that he was in his sixth decade. He grunted as he ignored the aches, heaved on the rifle and struggled to his feet.

Two riders crested the hill and reined in about fifteen feet away. Dust swirled at the horses' hoofs.

Abner's eyes narrowed; even with his spectacles, his eyesight wasn't so good these days. 'What can I do for you fellers?'

Their six-guns were holstered, high on their hips. The faces of both riders were concealed by the shadow from their hats. The one on the left leaned on his cantle, said, 'Just passing through.' He smiled, a strangely insincere white in the shade. 'My name's Justus Meak.' He gestured at the man beside him. 'This is my brother Gideon.'

'Meak? Name seems familiar, but can't place it,' said

Abner, levering a shell into the breech.

Gideon gentled his horse a few paces closer. 'You're Abner Nolan, ain't you?'

'I might be.' He half-raised the weapon, cautious, ready but not yet threatening.

Justus said, 'Your son said we'd find you up here with your wife.' He nodded at the grave, removed his trail-dusted hat. He had short black hair. 'Sorry she's dead.'

Abner relaxed, lowered the Spencer and smiled. 'That's right decent of you to say so.'

'My brother's sorry since it means we only get to shoot you, not her,' said Gideon.

'Yeah, annoying, that,' Justus said.

Cold fear clutched his heart as Abner hefted the rifle.

His hand a blur, Justus drew his six-gun and fired two shots before Abner levelled his weapon.

The slugs hit him in the belly and he stumbled backwards in shock. He let off a shot, the bullet ricocheting off stones round Ellie Rose's grave, and slumped onto the mound of earth, an arm draped over the headstone. Gasping for breath, he wheezed, 'Why'd you want to kill me – and my wife?' As he felt life ebb from him, a horrible taunting fear screeched inside his skull. 'My son, Rick – you haven't. . . ?'

'We sure have, old timer,' Justus said.

'I used a knife, so it was quiet like,' said Gideon. 'He's gone to meet his ma.'

'In God's name, why?'

Justus snarled, 'The Meak family owes you – and your pals for Bur Oak Springs – every damned one of you!'

'But my son, he—'

Gideon sneered. 'You and your pals didn't care about kids back then, did you?'

48

Abner didn't have an answer. What had kids to do with what happened at Bur Oak?

'Now,' Gideon said, leaning on the saddle pommel, 'are you going to tell us where you hid your share of the loot?'

'Loot?'

'Yeah,' Justus said, 'since it's obvious that you haven't spent it on your homestead!'

He shook his head. He was still wearing his eyeglasses, yet his vision was blurred, but it wasn't the tears of pain and frustration, he knew. He was done for and it irked him. He'd thought that with the new century so close, life out here in the West would be tamed, a place where their son could make his mark. Now, it wouldn't happen. Rick's inheritance was death.

'He ain't talking,' snapped Gideon. 'You shouldn't have shot him till he talked!'

'We know where Ransom lives,' Justus snarled, brandishing a handful of letters. 'The rest is easy – we make him or his family tell us.'

'But, there is no loot,' Abner wailed. 'This is madness! I don't know what you're talking about!'

Gideon swerved his horse round. 'Tough luck, old timer. Don't worry none, you'll soon be joined by all your pals in Hell!' He spurred his mount and the horse kicked dust in Abner's direction.

'Aye,' bawled Justus, urging his horse after his brother's. 'It's just like Ma said, the Meaks shall inherit the Earth!'

The brothers' laughter diminished, but the pain didn't.

When the two horsemen were out of sight, Abner hauled himself into a sitting position against the tombstone. He briefly raised his eyeglasses and wiped the moisture away, so he could see a little bit clearer, though he knew it wouldn't be for long. He took out his pencil and licked the stubby point, the iron taste of blood mixing with the lead. Slowly, ponderously, he opened the tin and scrawled a few words on the back of his final poem to Ellie Rose. Very soon, he knew, he'd join her.

Monday, 11 July

A rider raised dust as he approached the Bar-SR ranch and passed under the high wood shingle. 'Isn't that Sheriff Webb?' Adam said, leaning against the post of the porch.

Ransom slowly eased himself to his feet. The bandages had been removed that morning but the ribs still ached. He pulled the cigar from his mouth and blew smoke rings. 'Maybe he has news about the Calhouns.'

'Maybe,' said Adam. 'Seems in a hurry.'

'Howdy, Sam,' said the sheriff as he reined in at the hitching rail. He nodded at Adam: ' 'Mornin', son.'

'Good morning, Skip,' Ransom said.

The sheriff dismounted. 'It gets hotter every day, you reckon?'

Ransom nodded. 'And there's been no let-up. Worrying for the cattlemen if it continues like this.' Ransom gestured with his cigar at the bench seat. 'Come on up and rest your legs.'

'Thanks.' The sheriff climbed the wooden steps and wiped his face with his bandanna.

'Lemonade or coffee?' Ransom offered.

'Coffee'll be fine, thanks,' he said and lowered himself on the bench.

'Go tell your mother,' Ransom directed Adam.

'Sure, Pa.'

As Adam hurried indoors, Ransom sat beside the sheriff.

'Now, Skip, what brings you out here?'

'This.' He thick fingers delved inside his leather vest and withdrew a telegram. 'It's marked urgent, so I brung it, rather than let it wait till your next trip to town.'

'That's good of you.'

'Well, after the unpleasant mess with Wes Calhoun, I felt bad about that.'

'I understand, Skip. Politics.' He leaned forward and slit the telegram open with a finger. As he read the message, he felt the blood drain from his face and his stomach mangled itself into knots: ABNER NOLAN MURDERED. LEFT URGENT MESSAGE FOR YOU. PLEASE COME. MARSHAL JOHNSON, BETHESDA FALLS.

CHAPTER 6

COMES WITH EXPERIENCE

Ransom fastened his double holster. He noticed the buckle needed two less notches since he last wore the rig. He'd grown fat as well as old, it seemed. It felt strange, the weight of the two Remington six-guns on his hips after so many years. Strange but empowering. He shoved the last of his shirts inside the leather valise and turned to face his wife. She stood in their bedroom doorway, shoulder leaning against the jamb. 'Now, don't look at me like that, Charly.'

'What am I supposed to look like, Sam?' Tears welled in her pale blue eyes. 'I see you're wearing your guns. I thought you'd got rid of them.'

He smiled and slapped the double holster. 'Too valuable, honey. Anyway, it's just a precaution.'

'If Marshall Johnson hadn't put "murdered" in the telegram, I bet you wouldn't be taking any guns.'

Ransom shrugged. 'Maybe. Couldn't say.' He buckled up the valise.

'You're going after Abner's murderer, aren't you?'

He turned to her and shook his head. 'No, I'm simply going to see what's so urgent about Abner's message.' He pointed to the thin exercise book on the bed. 'Remember, we just got his book of poems less than a week ago.'

She nodded. 'I know. I read them – they're good.' She lifted a handkerchief to her eyes. 'You promise you won't go after his murderer?'

He limped across the room and embraced her. 'Of course I promise. I'm too old for that. Let the law deal with it. Anyway, maybe they've caught the culprit already.'

The landing floorboards creaked. 'Pa, can I come with you?' Adam asked.

Charlotte turned and sobbed.

Their son's face was earnest, the bruise over his eye quite mellow now.

Ransom stretched out a hand and rested it on his son's shoulder. 'No, Adam, I need you here. You're old enough to be the man of the house.' He tried to remember what he'd been doing at Adam's age; it was so long ago. Inwardly, he shuddered. Too damned dangerous, those days, yet he'd survived – thanks to a handful of good friends – and good luck, he guessed. Days filled with excitement, too; the young always hanker after thrills. 'Remember what I told you. Keep the shotguns to hand and loaded at all times.'

Charlotte gripped his bicep. 'Why are you saying that – just to alarm me?'

'No. It's what I do. A bunch of strangers could turn up any day, and they could be mean. I've always been prepared.'

'Don't worry, Pa, I'll be primed.'

Charlotte sobbed again as Ransom stepped back to heft his valise over his shoulder.

Jane joined them on the landing and the family descended the stairs without a word. On his way through their home, Ransom sneaked a glance, trying to fix it in his memory. He had an uncomfortable feeling in his stomach and wondered if he'd see the place again. Mentally shrugging off such negative thoughts at the door, he stopped and said, 'I reckon I'll be away a couple of days, that's all.'

'That's all the shirts you've taken?' Charlotte pointed out.

She'd no more think of him wearing the same shirt two days running than fly, he mused; not like those times before they were wed, when a shirt lasted a week or more.

'Just so,' he said. He smiled and hugged her then quickly embraced his children.

As he mounted his horse at the hitch rail, he noticed Charlotte turn and walk inside, her back hunched. Doubtless sobbing.

'See you on the fourteenth at the latest!' he called and waved to his children and urged his horse down the hardpan where not so long ago Sheriff Skip Webb had ridden up.

Sam Ransom passed under the Bar-SR ranch shingle and headed south to Bethesda Falls, wondering what business Abner had that was so urgent.

'It's a terrible business, Mr Ransom,' Marshal Johnson said, leaning forward on his lounge sofa. 'Abner's son Rick was cut up pretty bad by the killers. The doc reckons they did it before they shot Abner.'

'You're right, Marshal, it's terrible,' Ransom said. 'Rick was the same age as my son.' He shuddered involuntarily. He'd heard the expression before and hadn't given it any credence, but it surely felt like a ghost had walked on his –

or a family member's – grave. But it wasn't that preternatural chill that made Ransom feel uncomfortable. True, the room was cosy yet stifling, even with the open sash windows. But he suspected that his discomfort had nothing to do with the gruesome death of Abner's son, the heat or even this cramped room, but resided in the fact that he'd left Charlotte on less than good terms. 'Who found the bodies?'

'Reverend Higgins. He usually calls by to take them to church. Used to do it when Ellie Rose was alive and just kept on. Staunch church-goers, they were.'

Mrs Johnson entered the room with a tray of cups and a coffee pot. 'Here we are, Mr Ransom.' She was a good few years older than her husband, with long frizzy ginger hair going to grey. Despite the diagonal scar below her nostrils and across her plum lips, she appeared attractive. Maybe it was her blue jay eyes.

'Thanks, ma'am.'

The marshal briefly touched her hand. 'Thank you, Ruth, dear.' Then she left.

'This is the urgent note,' Johnson said, handing it over.

On one side of the sheet was a poem to Ellie Rose, similar to those in Abner's exercise book. On the reverse, scrawled in shaky blood-tainted lettering: *Warn Sam Ransom, Bar-SR. I was shot by Meak twins. They blame Bur Oak Springs. Meaks are hunting down Sam and the others. None are safe. Protect the families.*

Only the first two letters of Abner's name completed the message.

Cold clutched Ransom's heart.

'I reckon I know about the reference to the Meak twins,' Johnson said. 'I got a cable warning me that Justus and Gideon Meak escaped their prison escort and were on the loose.'

'Any description?'

'No. Posters'll follow in the mail.'

'What were the Meaks put away for?'

'A long term for bank robbery.'

'Figures,' mused Ransom.

Johnson gave Ransom a quizzical look but got no further response. 'I confess, the rest of Abner's note is a bit of a mystery. While I see you're possibly at risk, I don't really know what he meant. Maybe you can enlighten me.'

'It goes back a long time, Marshal.'

'I guess Bur Oak Springs is a place and you know where it is, right?'

Ransom nodded. 'It's a ghost town. Was then, is now. Apt, I suppose. There are a lot of ghosts in that place. And some seem resurrected all of a sudden.'

'This isn't helping. Who are "the others", then?'

'Old friends.'

'You're still not helping, Mr Ransom.' Johnson let out a sigh of exasperation. 'How can I trace Abner's killers if you won't be a little bit more forthcoming?'

'You have the names of the killers. Justus and Gideon Meak. As for "the others", Marshal, they're my friends. And my responsibility. Besides, they live outside your jurisdiction.'

'Maybe, but I can telegraph the law officers in their towns.'

Ransom shook his head. 'Don't worry, I'll warn them to be alert.'

Johnson pursed his lips. 'That doesn't help me catch the Meak twins.'

'But until you told me today, I'd never heard of the Meak brothers.' Ransom stood. 'Anyway, they've probably left the county by now.'

Johnson joined him in the hallway. 'Where will you go?'

'Telegraph office.' Ransom retrieved his black Stetson from the rack. 'I'll send a few cablegrams then ride on to Rapid City.'

'To meet one of "the others"?' Johnson said and opened the front door.

'That's right. Rory Carter is an accountant there. Our family had a meal with him and his wife last week when we went to pick up mail and supplies.'

Tuesday, 12 July

Sweat and trail dust clung to his blue placket shirt. Despite the pounding heat, Sam Ransom smiled as he rode into Rapid City. He'd spotted Rory Carter standing outside the saloon, a hand over his forehead to shield his eyes from the sun's glare.

He waved and Rory acknowledged with a vague gesture.

Ransom reined in next to a palomino at the hitching rail. 'Howdy, Rory – didn't expect to see you again so soon.' He wiped his brow with his yellow neckerchief.

'Always good to see you, Sam. Seems mighty worrying.'

'It is that.' Ransom dismounted but left his walking stick in the bedroll. He stepped up onto the boardwalk and shook Rory's slightly gnarled hand. During his last visit he'd noticed that his friend's arthritis was quite advanced, even though Rory was some eight years younger. 'Does Emma know yet?'

'Yes, I showed her the telegram – not that you said much, of course!'

Clapping an arm round Rory's shoulder, Ransom said, 'Let's go in and I'll tell you what I know.'

'OK.' He checked his waistcoat fob. 'Though I don't want to linger too long – Emma's got a meal ready for us.'

'Agreed. But I need to slake my thirst after that ride. It's damned hot.'

'Let's go in, then.'

Limping beside Rory Carter, Ransom swung wide the batwing doors. Inside, it was muggy with cigarette and cigar smoke. They entered but nobody paid them any attention. Two men followed them in and made their way to the bar.

The long bar ran the full length of the room, on the right. The place was packed with men. A few waitresses and whores sashayed between tables, taking orders.

Wes Calhoun leaned his back against the bar and chatted to a man on his right. There was no sign of the Calhoun ramrod, Chad Burton.

Hot anger clutched at Ransom's stomach. He gritted his teeth and clenched his fists. He didn't want to be diverted by any prideful confrontation. 'Over there'll do,' he told Rory and directed his friend to a table near the saloon window.

Rory said, 'I'll get the drinks – what'll you have?'

'Beer.' Ransom sat with his back to the bar and kept his hat on. 'It'll be a mite cooler than spirits.'

'OK. Won't be long.' Rory left him to scrutinize the stained table top and ruminate on why he was here.

But he didn't get far in his ruminations as, moments later, a pair of dusty boots appeared in Ransom's vision, to one side of the table. 'Hey, aren't you the old timer who got in my way last week?'

Damn! Ransom removed his hat, put it on the table in front of him and looked up at Wes Calhoun. 'What of it, son?'

Wes hitched his gun-belt. 'I had to get my saddle

mended, thanks to you. You're a bit too handy with a knife.'

'Comes with experience, boy. Come to think of it, you're too free with your fists when your opponent's held back by hired help.'

Calhoun's face reddened. 'What are you saying, mister?'

'I'm saying you'd better run off now, boy, since your ramrod isn't here to hold your hand or keep me from seriously hurting you.'

Abruptly, Wes kicked away a chair and crouched, his hand hovering over the gun-butt at his hip. His close-set grey eyes glared. 'I see you're wearing a gun today,' he said. 'Go for it.'

'Hey, Wes, he's an old man,' said a nearby cowpoke, 'your pa wouldn't—'

'This has nothing to do with my pa!' he snapped.

Slowly, careful not to make his aches worse, Ransom got to his feet and eased his chair behind him. He leaned forward, his palms flat on the table. 'You don't want to be doing this, young man. You really don't.'

'Oh, yeah?' Wes reached for his gun.

And stared into the barrel of Ransom's Remington before he cleared leather. His face drained of blood as Ransom cocked the six-gun.

'Oh, God,' whispered Wes, his legs shaking.

'What's this, Sam?' said Rory Carter to one side, carrying two pitchers. 'I leave you for a couple of minutes and you get into a fight?'

Eyes not leaving Wes Calhoun's, Ransom eased the hammer forward and smoothly holstered his gun. 'I think the young oaf was leaving,' he said.

'But—' Wes began.

Rory lowered the glasses to the table and shook his gnarled hands, which were clearly in pain due to the effort

59

of carrying them. 'I'd take a hint if I was you, young oaf,' he said. 'If you really upset Sam Ransom here, he's liable to turn nasty.'

'But I'm not an oaf!'

'If Mr Ransom says you're an oaf, accept it.'

Wes Calhoun swallowed and backed off. 'You haven't heard the last of this, Ransom,' he snarled. He turned on his heel and barged out through the batwings.

Rory sat. 'What was all that about?' He sipped his beer.

'I had a run-in with him and his father's ramrod the day after you entertained us so royally. Actually, I came out of it badly. It wasn't my finest hour.'

'The ramrod got in the way, eh?'

'Yes. He works for Jackson Calhoun. I'd have thought the town would have been full of it.'

'I'm an accountant, not a newspaperman or gossip,' Rory said. He nodded at Ransom's gun-belt. 'You need Darby, if you want to spread the word about your gun-toting ways.'

'I'm wearing these guns for a reason, Rory, and you know it.'

CHAPTER 7

STURGIS
STOPOVER

Quincy Newton and Irvin Hardee leaned against the bar and watched Ransom and Carter talking at the table. Without turning, Quincy whispered out the side of his mouth, 'The Meaks won't like this one bit.'

'What?' Irvin asked.

'That's Ransom with Carter.'

Irvin's nostrils flared. 'So?'

'We were supposed to follow Carter, see where he went, what he did, so when the Meaks come into town they'd get the drop on him. They need to quiz the guy about the loot.'

'I know that. But why're the Meaks going to get upset?'

'It's as plain as the nose on my face. The Meaks have a big problem.'

'Yeah, Quincy, you have quite a nose,' Irvin said. Hastily, he added, 'I still don't get it.'

'Did you see Ransom draw?'

'No, he was too damned quick.' A finger nervously

traced his pencil-line moustache. 'One second his hands were on the table, next he had his hogleg on that mouthy kid.'

'And now he's teamed up with Carter. And as I said, that's not good.'

'Do you know them?' Ransom asked Rory, thumbing toward two men who approached the batwing doors. One was gangling with straw-coloured hair, the other willowy with coal-black hair.

'No, never seen them before. Why?'

'They seemed to take an uncommon interest in us.'

Rory finished his beer and lowered the glass. 'It isn't every day they see Sam Ransom in action, friend.'

'Maybe.'

'Let's go – Emma'll roast me alive if we're late for dinner.'

Roast chicken and potatoes, with a hill of beans: demolished. Ransom sat back in his chair and removed the linen napkin from his collar. 'Thanks, Emma, that was delicious. I'm stuffed.' Briefly, he eyed his gun-belt hanging on a hook by the dining room door. Maybe another notch will be called for tomorrow, he mused.

'Thank you, Sam. I'm only sorry you couldn't bring Charlotte and the children along this time.'

'Adam asked to join me, but I don't want him getting involved.'

She nodded, concern in her deep brown eyes. 'Have you heard from Jubal yet?'

'No. We checked at the telegraph office on our way here. It's very worrying.'

'What will you do now?'

'I'll get the train, go visit him.'

Rory moved his chair back, stood and cleared his throat. 'I'm going with Sam, dearest. He'll need an extra pair of hands.'

Emma glanced at her husband's arthritic hands. 'You can't hold your six-gun, Rory, let alone fire the thing.'

'I'll take the rifle.'

'You can't go.' She turned to Ransom, eyes pleading. 'Tell my stubborn husband he can't go with you.'

Ransom shrugged. 'I stopped telling Rory what to do a long, long time ago, Emma. Sorry. He's his own man.'

'He's my man – the only man I've got or want.'

'I should hope so, dearest.' Rory's grin seemed a little forced.

She glared.

'I must go. We may even be too late for Jubal and Darby.'

'What,' she said, her tone close to alarm, 'no response from Darby either?'

'No,' Ransom said.

'Let me come with you,' she said.

'I've no objection, but it's your call, Rory.'

Emma slammed her palms down on the tablecloth and stood, her cheeks flushed. 'I'm my own woman, I'll have you know, Sam Ransom, and I don't need my husband's blessing in this.'

With a reluctant shrug of his shoulders, Rory nodded.

Wednesday, 13 July

Sam, Rory and Emma boarded the Fremont, Elkhorn and Missouri Valley train destined for Sturgis and thence to Deadwood. Impressed with the livery, Emma accosted the passing guard and complimented him on his smart uniform with its bar and ball emblem.

He preened, 'Why, thank you, ma'am. I'll have you know that I've been chosen especially for this Dakota 400 because I know the history hereabouts.'

'Is that so?' Ransom said.

'Sure.' The guard glanced at their tickets. 'For example, the town of Sturgis was founded not so long ago, in 1878. It was named after Jake Sturgis, a lieutenant with Custer at the Little Big Horn.'

'That's most interesting,' Emma said.

'Have you seen a couple of twins lately?' Ransom asked. 'Men going by the name of Meak?'

'No, I don't recall those names. What do they look like?'

Ransom shook his head. 'Can't say yet. But there can't be that many twins travelling on your railroad.'

'True, I guess.' The guard shrugged. 'Sorry I can't help.' He smiled and half-turned. 'Excuse me, but I must get on – Piedmont's the next stop, by the way.' He moved along the aisle and flung over his shoulder, 'The town was only founded two years ago, but it's going to grow fast thanks to this here railroad.'

The journey was tense and short on small talk and Ransom almost wanted the guard to return and continue with his history lesson, anything to break into their thoughts. Almost.

Even the grandeur of the passing scenery didn't seem to affect any of them.

Ransom smoked a cigar and fretted over his last sight of Charlotte, her back to him, shoulders hunched. Today was his birthday, damn it. Last night, he'd noticed the small package tucked into the corner of his valise. Charly's present, a silver fob watch, inscribed *With love xxx*. She'd added a note: *Come back safe. Your Charly.* He looked out the window but didn't see much scenery.

On arrival at Sturgis, Ransom hired out a buckboard from the station livery. Emma sat with the driver while Rory and Ransom sat on the flatbed with their luggage.

It was a short ride into the town. In front of the hotel, Rory and Ransom clambered down. Rory walked round the rear of the wagon and lifted Emma onto the boardwalk. 'See you later, dearest,' he said.

Emma nodded, smiled, gathered her bustle and strode into the hotel.

The two men strolled along the boardwalk and found the barber's easy enough. The shingle declared, Jubal Baines, Haircuts and Shaves. It was shut, the *Closed* notice slightly askew. Ransom peered through the window. The place didn't look too welcoming, a thin layer of dust on the seats and bench. Maybe Jubal had been on one of his benders again? 'Let's try the saloon,' he said, pointing to the building a block further down.

The bald barkeep was rather surly, Ransom thought.

'Look, I sell liquor and beer, not information. Do you want a drink or not?'

'All right,' Rory said, 'set up two whiskeys.'

As the barkeep filled the glasses, Ransom said, 'Thanks.' He tossed the coins on the counter. 'Now, do you know the whereabouts of a barber called Jubal Baines?'

'Couldn't say. Don't need a barber, do I?'

As they left, Rory said, 'A bit odd, isn't it?'

'Why?'

'Well, Jubal liked his drink. I'd have thought the barkeep would know him as a regular customer.'

'Maybe he drank in one of the other saloons.' Ransom

gestured at the main street. 'I can see another three just from here.'

'Yeah, that's probably it.' But Rory's tone didn't sound too convincing.

'I don't want any more whiskey,' Ransom said, 'so let's make our next stop the sheriff's office.'

They'd introduced themselves and asked about Jubal Baines.

The gangling beady-eyed lawman said, 'Are you next of kin?'

Ransom felt his insides squirm and his flesh ran cold. 'No, just old friends. When did Jubal die?'

The sheriff consulted his ledger and glanced up. 'July 8. My condolences, gents.'

'Two days before Abner,' Rory whispered to Ransom. 'I don't like the sound of this.'

'Thanks, Sheriff. I take it no next of kin turned up for the funeral?'

'Nope. He's buried in Boot Hill but his possessions barely covered the cost of the coffin, so he didn't get a tombstone.'

'I'll buy him one,' said Ransom. 'Rory, let's go visit the mortician.'

After they'd made arrangements for Jubal's headstone, Ransom told Rory, 'Go back to the hotel and tell Emma what's happened.'

'What are you going to do?'

'I'll cable Darby and warn him.' He pursed his lips. 'And pray I'm not too late.'

Barely an hour later, the three of them finished their meal in the hotel restaurant.

Ransom looked up. The maitre d' was in a hurried discussion with the lean telegraphist. A few seconds passed and then the maitre d' walked over. He leaned down to Ransom's ear and whispered, 'There's an urgent telegram for you, sir. The infernal little man wouldn't let me bring it to you, so perhaps you would join him?' He cleared his throat behind a gloved fist. 'I'd appreciate it if you didn't disturb the other diners.'

'Thanks,' Ransom said and stood unhurriedly. There were only two other tables taken and the diners were deep in their own conversations.

He approached the wiry man.

'I brung the answer straight away, as you wanted,' the man said, proffering the cable.

'Much appreciated,' Ransom said and passed the man a dollar bill.

The cable man stood patiently, waiting, while Ransom unfolded the message sheet. Ransom was surprised to find it was virtually an instant reply from Darby. It seemed that Darby had been away collecting new printing machinery from the station when the first telegram arrived and he'd replied to Bethesda; it probably arrived after Ransom left. Darby ended, *Thanks for the warning. We await your arrival. Take care.*

Thank God, Darby and his wife were all right. Maybe this was a wild goose chase, after all. No, Abner's message had been clear enough. And, besides, he didn't believe his instincts were that wrong. He pulled out a folded sheet from his inside pocket and gave it to the cable man. 'Send this pronto.'

Nodding vigorously, the man took the sheet. 'Yes, sir.'

'Here.' Ransom flourished another dollar as incentive. 'Let me know when it has been sent.'

'Yes, sir.' He turned and left.

Heavy of heart, Ransom strode back to the dining table. He must go on to Deadwood. The message he'd given the cable man was for Charlotte, warning her and Adam to be vigilant. *I'm going to be a couple more days, but aim to be home on the 16th. Take care.*

Irvin Hardee and Quincy Newton approached the camp with care since they knew that the Meak brothers had itchy trigger fingers. Stopping his horse in the copse at the extreme edge of the firelight, Irvin called out, 'Hey, it's us!'

Over to the right, someone cocked a six-gun. Either Kimball or Ashby, since the twins sat in the full glow of the camp-fire.

Gideon and Justus stood up. 'What kept you?' Gideon demanded, emptying the dregs of a coffee mug onto the ground.

'Yeah, it was supposed to be a basic look-see,' Justus said. 'You didn't get into trouble?'

'No, nothing like that,' Newton said.

Ashby and Kimball emerged from the shadows, their six-guns holstered. They waved a hasty welcome that didn't show in their faces.

'Coffee just brewed?' Irvin asked.

'Yeah,' Justus said. 'Tie up your horses and then tell us what you found out.'

'It ain't good news,' Irvin warned, turning his horse away.

They led their horses to the picket line and dismounted. While they loosened the cinches, Newton whispered, 'Why'd you say that?'

'It's the truth, ain't it?'

'What's the truth?' demanded Gideon.

He'd soundlessly followed them here.

'I'll tell you when I've had my coffee,' snapped Irvin.

Over coffee, Irvin related what they'd witnessed.

'Seems to me they've been alerted somehow,' said Justus.

'Yeah,' agreed Gideon. 'But I don't see how they could guess.'

'They're armed,' Newton said.

'That Ransom was quick, very quick with his guns,' Irvin said.

'For an old man,' added Newton.

Justus glanced at his brother. 'Tyler's supposed to be a printer in Deadwood. Should we try him next?'

Gideon shook his head. 'I've a much better idea.'

'What's that, brother?'

'Ransom's ranch isn't far from here, is it?

CHAPTER 8

PLENTY OF BLOOD

Thursday, 14 July

The Fremont, Elkhorn and Missouri Valley railroad had arrived two years earlier in Deadwood and Ransom reckoned that in that time the town had grown bigger and uglier. Now it was a vast sprawl of buildings spread across the valley between sloping tree-clad hills.

Darby stood on the platform, waiting.

Gushing steam, the engine came to a halt.

Ransom waved from the top of the steps and climbed down first.

He noticed that Darby walked awkwardly, stiffly. His old friend was the same age, yet time had not been so kind, it seemed, his once-fluid movement now stilted. He had close-cropped grey hair, a thick drooping salt-and-pepper moustache and a broad flat nose. Darby held a black flat-brimmed hat in one hand and a Navy Colt was slung on his left hip.

'Good to see you, Sam,' Darby said, shaking hands, his

70

grip firm, the fingers ridged and hard.

'I'm glad to see you too, Darby,' Ransom said. 'Very glad.'

Darby's denim-blue eyes betrayed concern. 'Abby's been worried sick since we got your cable.'

'She has good reason,' said Emma as she and Rory joined them. They exchanged greetings, and then spontaneously, the three men embraced.

Rory said, 'Three of us left.'

'But they have to find us first,' Darby said.

'Or our families,' Ransom added ominously.

They passed the office of the newspaper, *The Black Hills Pioneer*, and the Gem Theatre on the corner. 'Business is thriving,' Darby said, indicating the posters advertising sensational vaudeville acts.

'Yes,' Ransom replied, nodding at the Belle Union Saloon on the opposite corner of Main Street, 'the good and the bad.' He stepped into the road and crossed to the east section of Liberty Street.

'Where are you headed?' Darby asked. He pointed down Main. 'We live off here, on Grand Avenue.'

'I'll just send Charlotte a cable,' Ransom said and strode past the saloon, a doctor's surgery and a jeweller's. He ducked into the post office.

After the meal, Ransom leaned back in his chair and lit a cigar. He glanced around at the high ceiling and ornate decorations of the Tylers' dining room. Clearly, the printing industry paid very well indeed.

'That was delicious, Abby,' Emma said.

Ransom let out a curlicue of smoke. 'Darby, can you join us and go back to my place?'

Darby's denim-blue eyes sought out his wife on the other side of the table. 'I don't want to leave Abby.'

'I'd appreciate her company,' Emma said and grasped Abigail's hand.

Abigail's eyes filled with concern. She glanced at her husband.

'But why your place?' Darby asked.

'You and Rory have your wives with you. I left my family behind. I don't want to sound alarmist, but since the Meaks haven't troubled you, it's possible that they might go to the Bar-SR next.'

'Oh, poor Charlotte,' Emma said.

'I'm sure she'll be OK,' Ransom said. 'Sheriff Webb'll look after them till we get back, I reckon.'

Charlotte and her son stood on the porch, the front and back doors of the ranch house wedged open to allow what little breeze there was into the building. She frowned as Sheriff Skip Webb rode under the Bar-SR shingle. Behind him, the sky was ablaze with a fiery sunset, scudding grey clouds tinged with luminous silver light. Another sweltering day destined to be followed by an uncomfortable clammy night. Every window was open, but that had little effect.

Foreboding clutched at her stomach and heart as she noticed that the sheriff's horse was lathered. His face was creased in concern as he dismounted. 'Sheriff, it's good to see you,' she said, biting back the old familiar fear that she'd thought had long ago gone away. Turning to Adam, she added, 'Tend to the sheriff's horse, son.'

Adam seemed reluctant to leave her, doubtless as curious as her about the sheriff's evening visit. Then he said, 'Sure, Ma.' He jumped down the steps and passed the lawman on his way up. 'Howdy, Sheriff.'

'Howdy, son.'

Adam led the horse toward the water trough on her left.

'It's a mite late to be visiting, isn't it, Sheriff?' she said.

Sheriff Webb pulled out a folded yellow sheet of paper. 'This is urgent, Mrs Ransom.' He handed it to her. 'Real urgent.'

She held onto the sheet; it felt as though it would burn her fingers. 'I appreciate you bringing it, Sheriff,' she said, her voice wary. *Please God, don't let it be about Sam!*

'You'd better read it, Mrs Ransom.'

Her fingers trembled slightly as she unfolded it. His name was the last word of the message. Sam was alive, that's what mattered. The words she'd feared were not there but, as she read the text, she felt a heavy stone lodge in her chest. *Abner and Jubal killed. Darby, Rory and me on our way back to you. Be vigilant. You and ranch at great risk.*

She clutched the hand holding the cable to her bosom. 'From your tone, I reckon you've read this.'

'Yes. That's why I brought it.' He glanced around. 'Where's Jane?'

'Out back, doing chores before supper. Will you stay for a bite to eat?'

'Well, thanks for the offer, ma'am, but I came out here to suggest all three of you saddle up and return to town with me. Now. Tonight.'

'That's a long ride at this time of night, Sheriff.'

'Maybe so, but I'd feel happier knowing you were safe in Rapid City.'

At that moment, Adam shouted, 'Ma, there are riders coming and they're kicking up a lot of dust!'

You and ranch at great risk. Sam's words of warning echoed in her head. 'Adam, get the shotgun. I'll go find Jane.' She turned to Sheriff Webb.

'I'll stay on the porch,' the lawman said, adjusting his holster belt. 'Don't you worry, Mrs Ransom. If they're troublemakers, I'll see them off.'

She nodded and a wave of relief washed over her. 'Thank you, Sheriff.'

Charlotte hurried round the sided of the house to the water pump, where Jane was filling a bucket. 'Jane, leave that for now.'

Jane let go of the pump lever. 'Ma?'

'We may have unwelcome company. Let's get inside.'

Once in the ranch house, she directed Jane to the south side to close all the windows, while she attended to the rest. The front door opened onto a hallway that ran directly through to the back door. Adam stood in the hall, loading the shotgun.

'Stay at the front door, inside,' she told him.

'Sure, Ma.'

On the right of the front door was the main bedroom, a dining room and, at the far end of the passage, the door into the kitchen. On the left, the lounge, whose internal doors opened onto two further bedrooms. If visitors stayed overnight, Adam gave up his room and slept in the bunkhouse. The gun cabinet hung on the hall wall, its door already open. She pulled down two Winchesters.

Jane joined her. 'What's happening, Ma?'

'It's probably nothing, but I intend to be careful, like your pa said.' She held out a rifle. 'Here, you'd best load it yourself.'

Grabbing the weapon, Jane nodded and took a box of bullets from the drawer at the base of the cabinet. Expertly, she loaded the gun.

Charlotte's fingers trembled; she envied Jane's firm, con-trolled actions. Fear for her children, she guessed. Stamp on it, she told herself, and loaded the weapon.

*

Holding the shotgun steady, Adam stood in the doorway, behind Sheriff Webb. He glanced to the left and right. Two rifle barrels jutted out from the windows of the dining room and lounge. A bird cried out back of the house. His hands felt moist with sweat as the six dust-covered riders approached.

They clumped into pairs and rode through the entrance arch, then spread out into a single rank and finally hauled on their reins and brought their mounts to a halt to the right of the well. As one, they rested their hands on their pommels, all within easy reach of their six-guns.

'What can I do for you fellers?' the sheriff asked, his hand hovering over the butt of his revolver.

'We're looking for someone, Sheriff,' said the man on the extreme right of the line of horsemen. He had long brown hair that covered his ears, a beaked nose, protruding lips and a pointed chin. 'Maybe you can help.'

'Maybe I can. But tell me, who's asking me for help?'

The man grinned. 'Justus Meak is my moniker, Sheriff.' He turned slightly in his saddle and gestured at the others, one by one. 'Gideon, my brother.' A twin, no mistaking that hooked nose. 'Quincy.' Gangling, with bulbous nose and straw-coloured hair. 'Wade.' Muscular and compact, favouring black clothes and leather and wearing a Derby hat with a feather in its band. 'Turner.' Big as an ox under a high-crowned Mexican hat. He chuckled, then added, 'And the youngster, Irvin.' Terrible blue eyes; three fierce-looking scars on his face.

'Pleased to meet you all. I'm Sheriff Webb. The law in these parts.'

'Well, Sheriff,' Justus said, 'we'd like to chat all night, but we have things to do.'

'Such as?'

'Taking a hostage or two, as it happens,' said Justus Meak.

Adam felt a chill run through him as Quincy went for his gun.

Sheriff Webb cleared leather and shot Quincy in the chest. Almost in the same instant, Adam fired a single barrel at Quincy.

Quincy tumbled backwards off his horse, his weapon letting off a single shot.

The bullet sliced into Adam's thigh and sent him crumpling to the wooden boards of the porch, intense pain slicing through him. His knuckles whitened as he gripped the stock of the shotgun.

Suddenly, the air around him was filled with the sound of thunder and gunsmoke as pistols and the Winchesters blasted.

Through tear-filled eyes Adam saw the other five men dismount and scramble left and right.

Tugging the shotgun with him, Adam crawled to the door and it creaked open. 'Oh, Adam,' his mother moaned, and he felt her strong hand grip his collar and tug him through the gap. He let out a yell as his wounded thigh hit the doorpost. Sweat and pain swamped him. Using his good leg, he shuffled inside and the door slammed shut. Dazedly, he saw Jane above him. She pushed down on the wooden bar and effectively locked the door.

He glanced down and shuddered: his leg looked bad. Plenty of blood. Plenty of pain. 'Where'd they go?' Adam croaked.

Jane answered, her voice surprisingly steady. 'I saw one move over to the barn, another to the side of the house. He started shooting at the bunkhouse doorway.'

'The hands're trapped,' said Ma, kneeling at his side.

'Remember, the back door doesn't open.' She tore at the pants leg around the bloody bullet wound.

'Ow!' He swore. 'I knew we should've fixed that door – the hands've complained about it often enough. Said it's a route march round the back to the privy.'

'The wound's clean,' Ma said, 'the bullet didn't go in, glanced off.'

He winced. 'Glad to hear it. What about the sheriff?'

Ma let out a sob. 'He's a goner. At least three of them gunned him down as they got off of their horses.' She glanced up at Jane.

'I think I winged one of them,' Jane said, 'but can't be sure.'

'You'd better go back to the dining room. You can cover that side from there.'

'Right, Ma.' With a swish of skirt, Jane hurried from the hallway into the passage that led to the kitchen. From there, the door accessed the dining room.

'I'll go to the kitchen window, Ma,' Adam said, hauling himself up.

'You sure?'

'Yes, I'll be fine.' He hesitated in the passage. 'What did they mean – taking hostages?'

Jane fired her rifle from the window of the dining room, the report loud.

Ma shrugged. 'I don't know, son.'

He shrugged. 'Well, whatever, they're going to be disappointed.'

CHAPTER 9

GOING FOR A RIDE

Her heart pounding with a mixture of fear and pride for her children, Charlotte returned to the lounge and resumed her position at the window by the door. She fired at the one called Irvin, who hid behind the stone well out front. From time to time, he took pot shots with his pistol, the bullets peppering the front door, but otherwise seemed to be sitting tight, as if waiting for something to happen. Irvin let out unnerving whoops of joy and swore at the top of his voice between bouts of firing back. She had to confess that, even without the threat from his gun, his behaviour was unsettling.

As the minutes climbed, the lounge felt oppressive, with gunsmoke and heat. She felt her clothes clinging to her body. Whether it was sweat from the confined airless conditions here or her fear, she didn't rightly know.

The whole house was stifling, and in real want of a cool draught of air.

She heard Adam blasting at the man called Wade, who hid round the side of the stables. It seemed that Wade had taken his rifle with him, and fired back, his aim shattering the glass of the dining room windows. She feared for her crockery, inherited from her grandmother; it was her pride and joy, and thus displayed on the dresser against the eastern wall – in direct line with the window. But possessions were the least of her concerns right now, she thought, and let loose another volley at Irvin.

What did they want?

Hiding behind the woodpile at the northern end of the house, Turner Kimball kept the hands in the bunkhouse pinned down with ease. He only had to fire his rifle intermittently: each time there was any movement at a window shutter or the front door by the horse trough.

Justus tapped him on the shoulder. 'You're doing fine, Turner,' he said. 'Me and Gideon will soon put an end to this.'

Then Justus Meak slunk away in the direction of the outhouse.

Gideon trampled over the kitchen garden, his big feet carelessly crushing vegetables as he went. He brandished a Bowie knife and smiled at his brother who hovered by the window on the other side of the back door. Justus waved, signalling that he was ready. Gideon acknowledged his brother and then stopped at the window overlooking the vegetable patch. He leaned forward, and used his knife to break the latch of the window.

Stealthily, Gideon eased the shutters back and shoved open the window. It moved slowly but didn't make any sound. He heaved himself up to the sill and swung his leg over and within seconds he'd entered what appeared to be a bedroom. There was only one door, to his right. Judging by the layout of the place, the door led into the hall – which in turn led to the front and back doors. He felt his heart pounding and liked it. The anticipation of using his knife on someone yet again swelled in his chest. He moved to the door then remembered, and stopped. He returned to the window, leaned out and gave Justus the signal.

Justus raised his rifle butt and slammed it against the shutter of the back window. The wood creaked and groaned and glass broke noisily behind it.

He grinned and hammered the butt forcefully yet again. Wood splintered, loudly. For good measure, he shouted, so everybody could hear: 'I'm nearly in!'

Leaving a trail of earth clods on the floor, Gideon hid behind the bedroom's slightly open door. He grinned as he heard the racket that Justus made, which even seemed to carry above the sound of discharged rifles.

In one hand he held his knife, in the other, his pistol.

'Adam, they're at the back, if you can discourage them!' a woman's voice called from the front – probably the lounge.

'Right, Ma!' A youth's voice, to the left – from the kitchen end of the house.

Gideon slipped out into the hallway, his pulse racing.

Coughing on the gunsmoke, Adam limped down the passage and into the hallway. As he turned awkwardly towards the bedroom door, he sensed a movement out of the corner of his eye, but he was too late to react. The vicious blow slammed into the back of his head.

He sank onto his knees, his wounded leg stabbing fresh pain through his frame. He blacked out.

Mere seconds later, Adam recovered his senses. He was

surprised to find that he was standing, though on weak legs, and a man with bad breath and body odour supported him from behind. 'Don't make any sudden moves, boy, or I'll slice your gizzard,' the man snarled. He emphasized his threat with the blade of a Bowie knife at Adam's throat.

Adam croaked, 'Whatever you say, mister.'

'That's more like it. Now move, slowly.'

Adam did as he was told, and shuffled along the hallway, toward the front door, each step agony. His leg was excruciating, his head ached and he sensed an all-consuming fear in his gut that threatened to void his stomach's contents. He tried to fight it.

'Open the door,' the man demanded.

Adam extended a trembling hand, and pushed the lounge door wide.

Charlotte was at the nearest window, her face discoloured by smoke. She heard their movement and turned, her Winchester raised.

'Drop your weapon or the kid gets his throat cut!' snarled Adam's captor.

Charlotte recognized the man as Gideon, the twin of the gang's spokesman. When she studied his umber eyes, the colour of shadow, she feared for her life. Then she saw the blood trail down the side of Adam's head and the renewed bleeding of his thigh and let out a moan of concern. All the fight fled out of her.

'Jane!' she called, lowering the rifle to the floor. 'Drop your gun and come in here! Quickly!'

Empty-handed, Jane appeared in the hallway and stopped; she let out a shocked gasp.

'Join your mother, girl,' ordered Gideon.

Jane's lower lip trembled and her forehead creased. She hesitated.

'Jane, do as he says,' Charlotte said sternly. 'Please.'

At that moment, the front door succumbed to the weight of two men and crashed to the floor.

'About time!' Gideon shouted, and grinned.

Within minutes, the others, Wade and Irvin, joined them in the lounge, while Turner continued to pin down the bunkhouse hands.

Adam slumped in an armchair, and Charlotte knelt by his wounded leg, applying a fresh bandage. Jane sat on the chair arm.

Irvin strode over to Jane. 'I'll look after her,' he said.

Wade touched Gideon's arm. 'Not a good idea, boss.'

'Why's that?' Gideon demanded.

'Irvin Hardee's a multiple rapist. It isn't a good idea to put him anywhere near the women.'

'They're going to be dead soon anyway,' snapped Irvin, 'so what's it matter?'

Hearing this, Jane let out a wail of despair. Her mother comforted her.

Justus emerged from the bedroom that led from the lounge. 'That's where you're wrong,' he said. 'We need them.'

'Yeah, and I need them as well,' leered Irvin.

Wade butted in: 'What you said earlier, Gideon, I don't understand that. We never talked about no hostages.'

'My brother and I don't tell you everything.'

Justus sighed and pointed at the family. 'They're bait, you morons!' he snapped.

He glared at Irvin, his hand hovering over his holster. 'I suggest you back off. For your own good.'

Irvin raised his hands, palms out. 'All right. For now.' He eyed Wade. 'I'll remember this, gunslinger!'

Wade shrugged.

Justus signed to Wade. 'Put them in this bedroom – and tie them to the bed-stand.'

'What's this about bait?' Wade asked when he returned. Outside, Turner blasted away, keeping the hands pinned down.

'You'll see. Just be patient.' Gideon leaned toward a low coffee table. He picked up the cablegram lying there, and then read it. After a moment, he whistled.

'What's up, brother?' Justus said.

'Ransom and the others're coming back here.'

Justus grinned. 'That makes life easier for us. We'll just wait till they come.'

'No,' Gideon said, shaking his head. 'I have other ideas.'

'Such as?' Irvin sneered.

'A long ride.'

'What the hell. . . ?' Wade said.

'Where to, brother?' Justus asked.

'Bur Oak Springs.'

'Why?' Wade demanded.

'The loot, what else?' Gideon snapped.

Justus grimaced. 'It won't be there after all this time, surely?'

Wade gestured at the lounge. 'Look at this ranch house. Ransom's spent it long ago.'

'I don't think so,' Gideon said. 'The ranch is basic. Not ostentatious. If he'd had a share of all that loot, there'd be more to show for it than this.'

Irvin laughed. 'Who made you an expert on spending money?'

'Trust me on this.' Gideon winked at his brother then turned to Wade. 'Bring Mrs Ransom in.'

'Right, boss,' Wade said and turned for the bedroom.

'I'll go help,' Irvin said.

'No, you stay put,' Gideon growled. 'I don't want any tarnished goods just yet.'

Irvin faltered mid-stride. '*Just yet?* You mean. . . ?'

Gideon nodded. 'Maybe later, when we have Ransom and Carter.'

Irvin smiled and moved to one side, watching the door.

'What's that about Ransom and Carter?' Justus asked.

'Carter's with Ransom and Ransom will follow us.'

'So? How will they know where we've gone?'

'Mrs Ransom will leave them a note, that's why.'

'Then what, brother?'

'Then Ransom'll get what he gave our pa! A bullet in the back!'

Justus smiled. 'I like that part.'

They both turned as Mrs Ransom was led into the room by Wade.

'What do you want now?' she asked.

Gideon strode over to her and slapped her face. Not too hard, just an instructive blow.

Her eyes flashed but he noticed that she refrained from raising a hand to her reddened cheek.

'Ease on your tone, Mrs Ransom, and we'll get along fine.' He grinned and was repaid by a cold stare. 'I don't want to let Irvin here loose on your daughter – and the best way you can avoid that is to do as I want.'

She visibly paled, then nodded.

'We're going for a ride, you, me, your girl and my men.'

She gave a sharp intake of breath. 'What about my son?'

'He isn't fit to travel. He can stay. He can live; he'll show we mean business.'

He pulled out the cable sheet from his vest and turned it over, and flung it onto the coffee table. 'Write a letter to your husband.'

84

She darted a look at him, concern in her eyes.

'I know he's on his way here.'

'What do I write?'

'Tell him we've abducted you and your girl. He has till 21 July to come for you.'

'Come where?'

'Bur Oak Springs.'

She let out another gasp.

'You know it, eh?'

'No,' she lied, her voice croaking. 'I've heard of it – a long time ago.'

'Is that so?'

'Why there, why then?' she asked, her voice tremulous.

Gideon Meak's lips curved but it wasn't a grin, even if the yellow teeth were visible. 'Because that's where – and when – our pa was murdered by your husband, Mrs Ransom.'

'And that's where he and his pal Carter will die,' Justus added.

CHAPTER 10

UNCOMFORTABLY STRANGE

Friday, 15 July

The train shunted into Rapid City rail station, steam gushing across the platform. As the carriage juddered to a halt, Ransom reached up to the luggage rack and retrieved his hat. He glanced out of the window. 'Interesting,' he mused.

'What is?' Rory said.

'Welcoming committee.' He put his hat on and picked up his leather valise. 'I'll see you on the platform,' he said, and moved to the carriage door.

Steam fronds hovered over the platform like an early morning mist. A metallic-tasting clinging dampness touched his lips. His mouth was dry as he stepped down.

Three grim-faced figures emerged from the steam. He recognized Wes Calhoun and his ramrod, Burton. His body twitched at the memory of their last meeting. Then, he

86

hadn't been carrying. He surmised that the older man with the sour face was Jackson Calhoun. 'Good of you to wait for us,' he said, lowering his valise to the boards.

'My boy says you took a stick to him. Is that right, mister?'

'That's right.'

'Is that all you've got to say?'

'He's man enough to speak for himself, I reckon. What have you got to do with it?'

'If you hurt a Calhoun, you hurt all of us!'

'What a strange philosophy in this day and age.' Ransom shook his head, his eyes on Burton and Wes.

'Pa, let me take him, will you? I can do it!'

Ransom laughed. 'I don't think so. The last time he "took me", as he put it, he had his ramrod there to hold me down. Me, a man almost three times his age.'

Wes rushed forward, his hand darting for his six-gun.

Ransom leaped forward, his cane like a rapier, its ferrule jabbing Wes in the sternum, then flicking upwards, cutting the lad's chin.

Abruptly arrested in his attack, Wes fumbled at his holster.

Burton's hand closed on his pistol butt but he didn't move, his steely eyes staring behind Ransom.

Weapons cocked loudly at Ransom's back.

'Don't do anything you'll die to regret,' said Rory. 'This Winchester is darned difficult to control for my poor arthritic fingers.'

'Take charge of your son, Mr Calhoun,' said Darby. 'If you want him to live. My six-gun can make a mighty big hole in his guts.'

Wes backed away, one hand to his bleeding chin, another massaging his chest. His father pulled him to his side and his face darkened. He glared at Ransom then swung round and snapped at the ramrod. 'You're supposed to look after my boy, damn you, Burton! It's plain to me that you're not up to the job. You're fired!'

Burton pursed his lips, his cheeks reddening. He said, 'What about my pay, Mr Calhoun?'

'You haven't earned it,' Jackson Calhoun snarled. 'Get the hell out of town!'

Burton eyed Ransom. 'Your days are numbered, old man. Now, it's personal.' He swung round and strode toward the station exit.

Ransom smiled as Calhoun turned on his heel and, with one arm over his son's shoulder, followed after the sacked ramrod.

'Not the kind of welcome I had in mind,' Darby said.

'Me neither,' Ransom replied. 'But it isn't the Calhouns I'm worried about.'

They checked Rory's house and office and they were all relieved to find that the doors and windows hadn't been tampered with; both places were undamaged by intruders.

'Maybe it's not what we feared, after all,' Rory said.

'Yes,' Emma said, 'I'm sure it's going to be all right.'

Grimly, Ransom said, 'I hope so.' He eyed his friends. 'You don't have to—'

'No,' Abigail interrupted, 'we're determined to accompany you to your home.'

'That's right,' said Darby. 'And once we know Charlotte and the kids are all right, we'll probably avail ourselves of your whiskey.'

Ransom forced a laugh, but it was obvious that he was hurting, aching to be on his way.

'Let's get down to the livery and move out,' Rory said.

'Thanks, all of you,' Ransom said, anxiety heavy in his

heart, fearful of what they would find at the Bar-SR.

Saturday, 16 July

It was just past midnight when they rode under the Bar-SR shingle. Abigail tightly gripped the reins of the buckboard's two horses, while Emma sat beside her, anxious eyes scanning the ranch and outbuildings. Rory and Darby rode alongside Ransom, their horses skittish, probably catching the scent of the water in the trough by the porch.

Ransom's heart lifted as he spotted a single light flickering in the lounge window. 'Looks like someone's home,' he said, his tone edging a notch toward hope. Still, caution was called for, he reckoned. 'Darby, go round the back. Rory, check out the bunkhouse – the place seems too damned quiet.'

His two friends signed agreement and peeled their horses to left and right.

As Ransom dismounted his buckskin Bodie at the hitch rail, the signs didn't look that good. Nobody emerged from the house to greet him. He climbed the steps to the porch and noticed that there was no front door. His heart sank. 'Charlotte, Jane, Adam!' he bellowed.

'Pa!' It was Adam's voice and he felt a massive surge of relief. He rushed through the splintered doorway, noting the door was upended on the right, resting against the wall of the hall. Light flickered over the floorboards through the open lounge doorway. He rushed in.

And his heart seemed to stop for an instant. 'Adam!' he croaked, unable to move. Most of the furniture had been tipped over and broken.

Adam sat in a leather armchair, both his knees bandaged

but bloody, his face in the shadow cast by Hank, their ramrod, who stood to one side.

Hank's features were always drawn, as if he carried the woes of the world on his shoulders. But now, those flickering dark eyes held profound distress and sadness. 'I'm sorry, Mr Ransom . . .' he mumbled, glancing at young Adam.

'Where are the men?' Ransom asked, his face tense, eyes on his son, not the ramrod.

'In the bunkhouse, Mr Ransom. Waiting for word from me.'

'You bandaged him?'

'Yeah, he was in a bad way.'

Ransom feared the worst and rushed to Adam's side. 'Son, what have they done?' Then he noticed the harsh knife cut gouged in the boy's left cheek; it looked like the letter 'G'.

'I'm all right, Pa,' Adam whispered, his voice weak.

'But – your legs, they're—'

'One of the gang leaders shot my kneecaps, Pa.' He hissed in a breath, and added, 'It hurts like hell.'

'Did the Meak brothers do this?'

'Yes, the one called Gideon. You know them, Pa?'

'No, never met them, son. But we reckon they killed two of my friends.'

At that moment, Darby entered, followed by Emma and Abigail. 'Nobody out back, Sam,' Darby said.

Ransom let out a small sigh of relief. He'd feared what Darby might have found there.

Then Emma gasped. 'Oh, Adam!'

Ransom raised a hand, keeping his friends back.

Shakily, Adam clasped Ransom's arm. 'They took Ma and Jane.'

Ransom let out a groan between clenched teeth. If their

bodies weren't out back, it seemed most likely. 'Did they say why?'

'One of the leaders, Gideon, he shot my legs, said that way I couldn't follow them. He gave me this note from Ma.' He handed over the cable message.

Gritting his teeth, Ransom read Charly's words, then he looked up at his friends. Rory now stood at the doorway and behind him were the Bar-SR hands.

His facial muscles tense, Ransom grated, 'They're using Charlotte and Jane as bait – at Bur Oak Springs.'

Darby swore and quickly apologized to the women. Then he said, 'Why there, Sam?'

'Surely this has nothing to do with Braxton?' Rory added.

'Maybe it has – maybe it hasn't. I aim to find out, though.' Ransom turned to his ramrod. 'Hank, how many men have you got?'

'Four. The rest run off as soon as it was clear, said they had no stomach for gun-fighting.' He shrugged. 'The boys weren't able to fight back. We were all pinned down in the bunkhouse.'

Ransom stood up. 'It served no purpose for you all to get shot up, Hank.' He put a hand on the ramrod's shoulder. 'I appreciate what you've done.' He gestured at Adam's bandages. 'Can you get Adam back to town? He needs to see Doc.'

'Sure, Mr Ransom. I'll detail off—'

'No, I want you to take Adam in the buckboard. With two of the men as guards. And the ladies, of course.'

'Now, just a minute, Sam Ransom,' Emma butted in. 'We didn't come here to be sent off to a comfortable bed while our men-folk risk their lives.'

'That's the way it used to be,' suggested Rory.

'Maybe so,' Emma said, 'but that was then.' She moved

her hands to her hips, arms akimbo. 'This is now, and we're staying with our men. Isn't that so, Abby?'

Abigail nodded. 'I reckon.'

'Honey,' said Darby, 'I'd feel a lot better if I knew you were safe in town.'

Shaking her head, Abigail clasped Emma's hand. 'And I'd feel a lot better knowing I might be of use to Sam's wife and daughter, when we find them.'

Ransom's mouth twisted into the semblance of a grin. 'You might as well accept it, guys, this is one argument you ain't going to win.'

'Argument?' Emma said. 'Who's arguing?'

Ransom looked at his friends, then back to Hank. 'We're travelling light – and it seems we've got enough firepower.' His voice suddenly clogged with emotion. 'Besides, I don't want too many guns going off with my women in the cross-fire.'

'Amen to that,' Abigail said.

'Hank, could you bring in our cases, please? I reckon we women'll need to change into more appropriate attire for travel.'

'Sure, ma'am.' Hank stepped out.

'It's going to be mighty strange, going back to Bur Oak Springs after all these years,' Rory said.

'Uncomfortably strange,' Darby added.

Friday, 21 July, 1866

While Ransom and Rory located the stagecoach and two passengers, one of them dead, Darby and Jubal split up. As the dawn light percolated through the derelict buildings, Darby moved like a ghost through the shadows of the southern side of the town. He passed through a saloon – the name over the bar announced, The Real Golden Nugget! – and he was surprised to find that the tables and chairs were dust shrouded, covered in cobwebs. He shouldn't have been surprised, but he'd never entered a ghost town before. Behind the bar were a half-dozen ancient bottles wrapped in insect gauze. A beam of sunlight slanted through a gap in the ceiling and liquor gleamed in one of the bottles. He licked his lips, sorely tempted, then moved to the batwing doors. Time for a drink later, when the job was done.

The hardpan of the street was dotted by sagebrush. The only marks in the dust were made recently by carriage wheels, leading to the eastern end of town. Probably the livery. Move left or right?

He chose left and, pistol drawn, he trod with care along the boardwalk. Nothing seemed to stir, as if even a breeze couldn't find entry through the gorge. He felt sweat soaking the fabric of his shirt at his back by his belt. Jubal was checking the northern side, but he couldn't hear him. Maybe that was a good sign. Unless some of the stage robbers had silenced him. . . .

Suddenly, he started at the sound of gunfire, further up the street, and rushed to stand with his back against the plank wall, his pulse racing. He seriously considered leaving this town, this mission, and going home. He'd been sparking with Abigail, the schoolteacher, and he wanted nothing less than to find a trade and have children, anything to get away from desperadoes and gunfights. He shrugged off the thought and slunk along the boards, each creaking footstep seeming to announce his presence and presage his demise.

The shots came from a gaudy red and yellow painted place with faux pillars of wood, rather than stone. Desiré's Den, said the sign over the entrance. Windows by the door were shattered, the glass spread on the boardwalk.

Hunkering down, he peered through a broken pane.

Two men were strung upside down from a chandelier in the foyer. They were both very recently dead, blood dripping onto the carpet. The walls seemed to reflect the goriness of the scene, red flock with unlit bronze oil-lamp sconces. He'd never thought about it before, but now he wondered if whorehouses favoured red decoration to celebrate the death of a maidenhead, or something else entirely different.

At the plush bar counter, two men laughed and supped from the shattered necks of liquor bottles.

Two less, Darby reckoned.

He entered the swing doors of the abandoned bordello and said, 'Had a good time?'

Both men whirled round, instantly realized Darby wasn't one of their gang, and went for their guns.

Clearly, they were incapable. But Darby had no qualms about shooting drunks. They'd cold-bloodedly murdered two innocents – probably hostages. He raised his Navy Colt and shot them both before they could clear leather. As the sound of the shots diminished, so did the crash of glass bottles. Darby felt good about that. Two bad guys sent to Hell.

He wondered how many more were left. The shots of these two didn't seem to attract any attention from their pals; he could only hope that none of the gang would now come to investigate. Keeping one eye on the doorway, he knelt by the two corpses and searched their clothing. Usually, everybody carries something to identify them – whether it's a daguerreotype from home, a purchase receipt or an old crumpled letter. He found that he'd killed Joe Goggin and Pat McKean. 'Never heard of them,' he said and stood up.

Abruptly, the chandelier's fixture to the ceiling made an alarming sound and the whole thing plummeted to the floor, directly on top of Goggin and McKean. In the same instant, Darby leaped over the counter and hid as shards of glass and candles flew in every direction.

Maybe that goddamned ruckus would bring his pals? He waited, tense, for about five minutes, but nobody stirred outside. He licked dry lips.

The spirits behind the counter tempted him. Again, he licked his lips. Get behind me, Satan, he thought, remembering Abby back home. She said more than once that he was getting as bad as Jubal with his liking for liquor. Unjustified, but he still reckoned that this was definitely his last job. He'd resign when it was over.

It was over for Alvin Forrest and Tim Burnside, too, as Ransom and Rory recognized the two men approaching the livery stable. The gunfight was swift and one-sided. It was obvious that Forrest and Burnside hadn't anticipated any danger, while Ransom and Rory had. As soon as the two men slumped dead to the hardpan, Ransom signed to Rory his intentions.

Rory nodded and readied himself with the Winchester.

Ransom limped hastily across the street to the Cavendish Hotel next to the assayer's office. He entered, alert, wary, and climbed the staircase. Moving along the landing, he used his good leg to kick in several room doors but nobody hid inside. There was another staircase, he noticed; perhaps leading to the roof or an attic.

Then he heard Rory shouting his name.

He hurried to the nearest window that overlooked the main street.

Rory called, 'They're getting away!' And he pointed

towards the west.

Two horsemen urged their mounts from behind the furthest dwelling.

Darby emerged from the far building on this side of the street and started firing his six-gun, to no effect.

Ransom exited the room and ran up the next staircase and came out on the roof. From here, he had a perfect view of the western end of the basin. He felt his heart lurch a little as he recognized Braxton astride one mount. The other man wore a black sombrero – probably Pascoe, then.

Abruptly, disconcertingly, Braxton shuddered in the saddle, then he hunched forward, and the horse kept on running towards Narrow Gorge. But Pascoe slumped, his sombrero toppling. The explanation came seconds later as the double boom from Abner's gun crossed the basin. Ransom watched as Pascoe slid off his saddle, one foot caught in a stirrup; he was dragged about half a mile before the horse halted.

Afterwards, they used the shovel from the stagecoach to bury Mr Hearst, the driver and the other passenger in the cemetery at the east end of the ghost town. 'The bodies of the gang can stay and rot,' Ransom said. 'We're not sweating over them.'

CHAPTER 11

BAD MEMORIES

Sunday, 17 July, 1892

Justus pulled up his horse and stopped as the last punishing rays of the sun lit up a flat rocky area on the edge of a scrawny copse of willow and thickets of chokecherry. 'We'll make camp here for the night,' he said.

Astride Jack, her palomino, Charlotte heaved in a sigh of relief. There'd been no respite from the sun. Her head ached and her clothing felt uncomfortably wet. She glanced over at Jane on her sorrel and fought back tears. Jane's face was blotchy with sunburn and her eyes seemed deadened, the sockets empty.

Gideon said, 'That damned sun's dried up enough wood for a fire. We'll get there day after tomorrow, I reckon.'

'Seems a long ways to go,' Wade said, wiping his brow with a cloth. 'Especially when we could've just waited for Ransom and Carter at the Bar-SR.'

'Seems to me, you're getting a bit uppity,' Gideon said, fingering the hilt of his knife.

'No,' Wade replied hastily, 'just thinking aloud what the others're thinking.'

'Hey,' snapped Irvin, 'don't bring me into this, you bastard. You sure as hell don't know what *I'm* thinking!'

Wade laughed. 'No? I bet ten dollars you're thinking of having a piece of that young girl!'

Irvin's nostrils flared and his scars turned livid.

'That's enough, the pair of you!' Justus ordered. 'The girl will be unharmed till I say different!'

'Well, don't forget to say,' mumbled Irvin as he turned on his heel and stormed over to his saddle and bedroll.

'Let's get grub organized,' Gideon said. 'Wade, gather firewood. Turner, get the victuals out. Irvin, go guard the trail.'

'I've just got settled,' Irvin said from his bedroll.

'If you want to eat, do as my brother says,' Justus said.

Grudgingly, Irvin stood with his rifle and strode back the way they'd come.

Gideon walked over to Charlotte and Jane. 'Here, let me help you ladies down.'

'We can manage,' Charlotte said. Tethered hands gripping the pommel, with a flurry of skirts, she swung a leg over the saddle and dropped to the ground on both feet. Jane did the same. 'We don't need any favours.'

Gideon grinned. 'I reckon you do, if you don't want Irvin let loose on either of you.' He smiled and drew his revolver, aimed it at Charlotte. 'In fact, I've got to thinking we only need one hostage to draw Ransom into the trap.'

Justus stepped forward and raised his hand in front of the weapon. 'No, brother, we need both.'

'Why?'

'We might have to split up. Or there may be more shooting than we bargain for, and one of them might get killed. Two improves our chances of at least one of them coming out alive to serve as insurance.'

Shrugging his shoulders, Gideon holstered his gun. 'Yeah, you're probably right.'

'I usually am, brother.'

The women had their left wrists tied to a tree, so they could eat and drink one-handed. The chow – corned beef hash – was burned in places, and the coffee was powerfully strong, but Charlotte swallowed her share without complaint. She needed to keep up her strength, not just for herself but also for Jane.

Worry sent her stomach into somersaults. Jane seemed despondent, justifiably fearful.

She remembered all those years ago, when Sam had rescued her. Then, she'd really believed her life was about to end.

Moisture rimmed her eyes and she blinked it away. Be strong, she told herself. She caught Jane looking at her and smiled. Jane's response was a weak flicker of her lips, but her eyes seemed fatalistic, as if she already saw her own death.

Later, their wrists were retied and they lay on separate blankets, their saddles for headrests. Although she didn't think it possible, Charlotte fell asleep.

Scuffling and shouting from Jane's bedroll startled Charlotte awake. In the faint moonlight, two men stood over Jane, fighting. Terrified, Jane hunched up on the ground, her eyes huge with alarm.

Suddenly, Irvin let out a terrible scream and slumped sideways. Gideon thrust him away and the man fell hard to the earth. He rolled onto his back, a knife protruding from his chest, and lay still.

Charlotte crawled over to Jane, clasped her daughter's hand, but didn't dare say a word. She put a fingertip to Jane's trembling lips and shook her head, trying to signify that it was going to be all right now that Irvin was dead.

Kneeling by the body, Gideon withdrew his knife and wiped the blade on the corpse's clothing. 'Should've done as my brother told you,' he growled and stood up.

Wade said, 'You mean the fool tried to. . . ?'

'Yeah,' Gideon said. He grinned at Charlotte. 'Me, I prefer older women.'

Charlotte shuddered.

'Leastways,' Turner said, 'that's one less to share the loot. And we've got a spare horse and saddle.'

Monday, 18 July

Their trek was much the same as the day before. The sun beat down on them, remorseless, draining the moisture from their bodies. From time to time, beyond Turner and Wade up ahead, Jane pointed to the odd mirage, like a tantalizing pool of cool water, and licked her cracked lips. But Charlotte knew better. 'Trick of the light,' she whispered dryly. 'In this kind of heat, the mind plays tricks.'

'I don't know if I can go on much further, Ma,' Jane said.

Charlotte pointed to a cluster of blue-white beardtongue in the shade of a gnarled solitary maple tree. 'See, even in this heat, those wild flowers survive.'

Jane glanced at the flowers without interest. 'I don't think they're going to let us live, no matter what happens.'

'Courage, my girl. Your father will rescue us, I'm sure.'

'I'm aching all over.'

'Me too. But be strong, Jane. We can rest when we get to Bur Oak Springs.'

'That's what I'm worried about, Ma. Eternal rest. I don't want to die there – or anywhere right now. I've got my whole life in front of me yet.'

'We'll survive. Remember Adam – he was brave, too.'

'Oh, Ma, I'm so sorry I'm whining. You're right. He must've been in awful pain.' She wiped the heels of her hands against her sweating brow. 'Maybe it's the heat getting to me.'

'The heat does that, sometimes,' Charlotte said, thinking about Bur Oak Springs.

She turned in her saddle and called to Justus Meak, 'I heard one of your men talk about sharing the loot – that wouldn't be the gold from the stagecoach robbery in 1866, would it?'

'It might,' Justus replied, geeing his horse to ride alongside hers.

'There was no loot,' she said.

He leaned to one side, his face screwed up. 'You're a liar.'

She shook her head. 'Braxton and his men were all shot up. The lawmen found no loot. Only Braxton got away, though wounded. He must have taken it.'

Gideon drew up on the other side of her. 'Is this true, brother?' he asked.

'Of course it isn't. D'you think we'd have lived our lives so poor if Ma'd got hold of the loot?' He stared at Charlotte. 'I don't know why, but she's lying.' He spurred his horse forward and called over his shoulder. 'And we'll find the truth of it when we get there!'

Darby rode point and was a good half-mile ahead of their

101

party when he spotted the badly constructed cairn of stones, the air above it abuzz with black flies. His mouth suddenly went very dry as he reined in and dismounted. The smell was familiar. He feared what he'd find. Maybe he should wait for Sam and the others. No, he'd better check first. He pulled up his bandanna to cover his mouth and nose, and then his gloved hands tugged at the stones.

Within a minute or so he'd uncovered the head of a man. He let out a sigh of relief. Thank God, it wasn't one of Sam's womenfolk. The dead man had a pencil-thin moustache and coal-black hair that was powdered with sand and dust. The grimace on the pale face suggested the man had died in agony. Serves him right.

Darby turned and walked over to his horse. The animal was skittish, as it had smelled death. He waved to Ransom and the others who were approaching, then led his horse to meet them.

'What's that?' Rory said, pointing at the disturbed cairn.

'I reckon it's one of their gang. He died in pain, if that's any consolation.'

'One snake less to worry about,' Ransom said.

'Darby, are you going to cover his face again?' Abigail asked from the buckboard. Both she and Emma looked somewhat younger in their tight-fitting jeans and white cotton shirts.

'No,' Darby said. 'Let the vultures have a feast.' He glanced up at black shapes that swirled in the clear blue sky. 'Snake is their favourite.'

Ransom shrugged. 'Let's get on, then. We've still got some way to go before we get to Bur Oak Springs.'

'I don't feel like riding point right now,' Darby said. He remembered how he'd feared whose body he might find under that cairn. He didn't want to be the one who discovered Charlotte or Jane's corpse, so he made up an excuse that happened to be close to the truth anyway. 'Talk of Bur Oak Springs brings back bad memories.' He glanced at Abigail and shook his head. 'Poor old Jubal.'

He remembered. He'd come out of Desiré's Den and crossed the street. Cautiously, he entered the printer's shop. Now, that was a useful trade, he thought. Later, maybe. He slunk through into the back office. Then he saw Jubal, chasing a huge man with a black beard. They both ran into a dwelling across an alley. Jubal fired a shot, but the fugitive kept on running. Then they'd passed out of sight.

He exited the printer's and stepped down to the alley.

Suddenly, over to his left horses whinnied and shots were fired. At the same moment, Jubal yelled and an almighty crashing sound came from the house at the end of the alley.

Torn, Darby moved to investigate his friend Jubal's situation, his pistol cocked.

He found Jubal and the fugitive, George Scott; both of them had fallen through the rotten floorboards of the house into a mine tunnel about twenty feet below. The bearded Scott had probably cushioned Jubal's fall.

Later, when they pulled Jubal out, they discovered he was suffering from a serious head wound. Jubal's memory was forever faulty after that day.

'Yeah, bad memories,' Darby said again.

'All right, I'll go on ahead this time,' said Rory, and he rode out.

The day grew even hotter and Ransom knew that it drained them all. Abigail moaned about the buckboard seat and her aching back. Emma tended to keep quiet, though she seemed tired and tight-lipped. Darby stopped several times to empty his weak bladder behind a cactus. 'Old age,' he complained to hide his embarrassment.

Presently, Rory returned. Without saying a word, he held out a shred of clothing.

Ransom took it and rubbed the material between fingers and thumb. 'Yep, that's from Charlotte's dress,' he said. 'She's leaving a trail.'

Tuesday, 19 July

Dusk was about to settle over the land when the Meak party arrived at the entrance to Narrow Gorge. The only road access to Bur Oak Springs was completely blocked by a massive slope made up of boulders and shale. 'Looks like explosives brought this lot down,' Justus observed.

Dark silhouettes of some kind of equipment were visible above, on either side of the scree. 'Machinery of some sort,' Gideon said, pointing.

A small corral stood empty. The ground all around was trodden flat. As far as they could see in any direction, small wooden pegs pierced the ground, suggesting rectangular shapes.

'Could be a survey going on here,' Gideon said. 'Looks like lots've been laid out for some kinda township.'

'Yeah,' Justus said. 'I reckon the workers for all this are in that tent town on the river we bypassed earlier.'

'Here, maybe this explains it,' called Wade. He pointed to a square notice nailed to a wooden post.

'What's it say?' Gideon asked, riding up.

'Can't rightly make it out,' Wade said.

Gideon laughed and pulled up his horse by the sign. 'Can't rightly read, more like, eh?'

'So?' Wade snapped. 'I'm a gun-for-hire, not a dad-blamed schoolteacher.'

'Yeah, right. I was forgetting.' Gideon leaned down and his lips moved as he read the sign. 'Says the town – Bur Oak Springs – is private property. And on 21 July the whole basin will be in-inun – inundated. So's it can be a reservoir for agri-cultural irrigation. Some kinda test case. Signed by Chief Engineer—'

'What's "inundated" mean?' Wade asked.

'Flooded,' said Turner.

'*What?*' yelled Justus.

'That's the day after tomorrow,' Wade said.

'I know that, wise-ass!' snapped Justus.

Wade shrugged. 'Well, the reservoir water's gonna cover up Ransom and his buddies – and his family. Real tidy, if you ask me.'

Between gritted teeth, Justus said, 'I didn't ask you, Wade. It'll also cover up the loot – for good!'

'Not if we get to it before then, eh?'

'Yeah, all right,' Justus said. He dismounted. 'We'll have to leave the horses. Turner, put them in that corral.'

'Sure. Then what?'

Gideon pointed at a rough goat-trail leading up the side of the butte. 'That's worth a try.'

Reluctantly, they all dismounted. They retrieved their water canteens, which they'd refilled at the river, and the rifles from their scabbards. While Turner took the horses to the corral, Justus led the way, followed by Charlotte, Wade, Jane and Gideon.

A few minutes later, Turner caught them up, and stayed at the rear.

By the time they reached the top, the last of the daylight barely permitted them a glimpse of the town. 'I've never been in a ghost town before,' Turner said.

'Arghhh!' Wade said.

Turner jumped, then scowled as Charlotte let out a short laugh.

'You fool,' Justus said. 'There are no such things as ghosts!'

'Quit that, Wade. This is serious business,' Gideon said and pointed. 'Down there. That's where Pa was shot. He was as good as killed there.'

'Yeah,' Justus said. 'We go down at dawn.'

CHAPTER 12

FULL OF GHOSTS

Wednesday, 20 July

Dawn light spread across the dry rugged landscape as Ransom and his company broke camp. Within half an hour, they were on the trail again, the rocky cliff walls getting closer. An hour or so out, their trail skirted a large tent town by the river. 'That's the river Buroak, according to the map,' Rory said. He gestured at the tents. 'The Meaks didn't want to go there, that's for sure.'

Even the town's temporary nature looked inviting, offering shade and relief from the brain-pounding heat and constant dust.

Ransom reined in and swung round in his saddle. 'Ladies, do you want to stop over and get refreshed? Maybe stay while we go on?'

Emma geed up the buckboard horses. 'We go where our men go, Sam. You should know that by now.'

'Thought I'd ask,' he said and urged Bodie forward.

Two more hours passed on the trail and it was mid-

107

morning when they arrived at the point where the entrance
to Narrow Gorge used to be.

Three men stood at the base of a massive rock-fall that
blocked the entrance. A small corral seemed tightly packed
with ten horses, seven of them saddled; three other saddles
were slung on the topmost poles. Above them, on the lip of
the bluff, men and machinery made a raucous noise.
Ransom heard a donkey boiler puffing away on steam somewhere up top.

He signed for the others to draw to a halt. 'Stay here – I'll
go and investigate.'

'I'll join you,' Derby said.

Ransom nodded and they rode side by side.

The three men wore dust-covered overalls.

'Howdy,' Ransom said, and reined in his horse.

'Howdy,' said a grey-haired stocky man with a bushy
moustache. 'What can I do for you fellers?' A big tall
bearded man stood behind him, watchful, a shotgun in the
crook of his arm.

'We were planning on going through that gorge – until
we saw it's blocked.'

'Yeah, sorry about that. You can't do that, the whole
basin's off limits.'

'Says who?' asked Darby.

The man thumbed his chest. 'Says me, chief engineer on
this project.'

A shotgun was levelled on Ransom and Darby.

'What project is that?' Ransom said.

'You're a mite full of questions,' the chief engineer said.
'Who the hell are you, anyway?'

Ransom grinned, dismounted and took off his hat, hung
it on his pommel. 'Name's Ransom. Used to be a lawman in
these parts. I've come visiting Bur Oak Springs for reasons

of . . . nostalgia.' He limped forward and held out his hand.

The chief engineer shook. 'Max Faust.' He gestured behind him. 'The guy with the greener is Hal Small.' He screwed up his eyes, studying Ransom. 'I think I've heard about you from the boss.'

'Really?' Arms akimbo, Ransom gazed up at the workmen on the top of the butte. 'Who's your boss?'

'Willis Hearst. I reckon you know him.'

Ransom let out a short laugh of surprise. 'Indeed I do! I'd like to meet him again.' He gestured at the men on the bluff. 'Is he here now?'

'Nope. He's due in tomorrow morning, just in time for the big bang.'

'Big bang?' queried Darby.

'We're flooding the basin. Diverting the river to do it. That's the project.'

Hal Smith lowered the greener, but Ransom noted that he stayed watchful.

Darby removed his hat and whistled. 'You're going to cover the town with water? All of it?'

'Sure,' Faust said. 'It's going to be a reservoir for the whole area. Wayne Hearst Lake.' He pointed at the many lot marker pegs. 'A new town is planned just about where we're standing: Hearst City.'

'What was wrong with the old town?' Ransom asked.

'It's full of ghosts. Besides, the boss says it has bad memories. He wants shut of it, for good.'

'Can he do that?' Darby asked and dismounted.

'Sure he can; he bought it. The town's now private property and visitors – for nostalgic or any other reason – ain't welcome. Belongs to Mr Hearst, lock, stock and barrel.' Faust indicated the wooden notice.

Darby and Ransom walked up to the board and read it.

'What do we do now?' Darby whispered.

Ransom bit his lip. He had no doubt that the Meak brothers had taken Charlotte and Jane into the town. 'Mind if we look around?'

'What for?'

'We've been tracking a party of people, and they came this way.'

Chief Engineer Faust nodded. 'I'd been wondering about that.'

'About what?' Darby asked.

Faust thumbed at the corral. 'When I got here from camp, we found those seven horses, all saddled up. No idea who they belonged to, neither.' He pointed to the goat trail, familiar to Ransom even after all these years. 'Their riders probably went into the basin using that track.'

Ransom said, 'Is it all right for us to go in after them? Being private land and all.'

'No, you can't do that. Sorry.' Faust hooked his thumbs in the pockets of his pants. 'Anyway, there's no need. I sent Algy, one of my men, to tell those guys to get the hell out of the basin pronto. Noon tomorrow we blow the dam. On the dot. And believe me, you don't want to be there when it gets flooded.' He pulled out his fob watch. 'Algy should be back with them in about an hour, I reckon. D'you want to wait?'

'I don't think your man will come out, Mr Faust,' Ransom said. 'The men who've gone into Bur Oak Springs are desperate and won't listen to Algy or anyone else, no matter what. I'm afraid Algy'll be dead already.'

'What the hell?' Faust's face reddened. 'What's all this about?'

'It's a family matter,' Ransom said. 'I really need to go in.'

Hal Small hoisted the greener again, clearly taking a cue

from the deteriorating tone of the conversation.

Faust shook his head. 'Nope, you can't go.' He chewed on his lip. 'If Algy's been murdered by those guys, then they've sealed their own fate.' He shrugged. 'This basin gets flooded tomorrow. On schedule.'

'But, Mr Faust,' Darby began, 'there's wo—'

'That's an order, mister!' snapped Faust, leaning with his face bare inches from Darby's. 'Anyone who trespasses gets shot!'

'But—'

Ransom grabbed Darby's arm and dragged him away. 'Let's do as Mr Faust says,' he said. 'The others are waiting.' He gestured at Rory, Emma and Abigail.

They both mounted up. Ransom nodded at the chief engineer. 'Thanks for your time, anyway, Mr Faust.' He swung Bodie round and rode towards the buckboard, Darby following a short distance behind.

Charlotte struggled to remain upright as she moved down-hill, her hands tethered together and attached to a rope that connected her to Jane. They had to be careful not to get snagged on the many old bur oak trees. From time to time, she steadied herself against a tree bole, though her fingers tended to slip on the velvety moss on the northern side of the ash grey bark. While the shade provided by the trees made life easier, she was still parched, her tongue almost stuck to the roof of her mouth. Worse, the slope amidst these trees was dried up loose soil, littered with acorn husks and dead saplings, and she slid and slithered repeatedly as her footing unexpectedly gave way. Dust disturbed by the Meak twins ahead sent her into a coughing spasm, but she dared not stop. Wade and Turner were close behind and were liable to collide into her and Jane.

Her knees jarred and ached but, finally, the pressure eased as their descent levelled off. Soon, they approached a rank-smelling wide pond. Over on the left was a decrepit water tower, beneath which grew a thick cluster of agaves.

They all stopped at the pool's edge. She wiped her mouth and sucked in air. She noticed that the men were not in much better shape. Wade seemed in a bad way; maybe his broken nose made it difficult for him to breathe when he was exerted. She had no sympathy.

Her stomach clamped tight as she watched the men swig from their water canteens. She turned away and reached out for Jane and hugged her. 'Are you all right?' she asked, her voice dry, like an empty riverbed.

Jane nodded, and offered a faint smile, but wouldn't or couldn't speak.

'Is this such a good idea?' Turner said, replacing the stopper on his bottle. 'I can't see Ransom and the others coming.'

Gideon growled an expletive and added, 'We're here to find the missing loot, remember – not just to get even with Ransom.'

'Yeah, I forgot,' Turner said.

'OK, let's get started.' Justus motioned at the eastern end of the pool. 'We go round here, and approach the town from that end.' He pointed to a two-storey building and opposite on the other side of the street, the taller livery stable. 'Work our way through from there till we uncover the loot.'

'That's at least twenty buildings to search!' Wade exclaimed.

'Well, the sooner we get to it, the better. We need to locate that loot before Ransom and his pals turn up tomorrow.'

'Maybe they'll be early,' Charlotte suggested.

Gideon grinned. 'I've thought of that, Mrs Ransom. One of us will stand sentry while the others search.'

'What about us?' Jane asked.

'You get tied up in the livery.'

'Where else?' Charlotte murmured, and wondered how she'd managed to end up precisely where she'd met Sam and in the same predicament twenty-six years ago.

'What did you say?' Justus demanded.

'I just meant the livery's a sensible place to keep captives,' Charlotte replied.

'What would you know about it, eh?' snorted Wade.

What, indeed! She shrugged, intent on concealing the fact she'd been here before. If they guessed that she'd been here at the time of Braxton's fatal wound, then they might figure she knew where the loot was, and that would prove difficult. She didn't reckon that the loot was still in the town, but they wouldn't believe her, she felt sure. And maybe they'd get rough with her to no avail.

'We'll locate the tallest building and post our lookout there,' Justus said. 'I don't want any surprises from Ransom.'

Once Ransom and his friends had ridden a mile or so to the east and veered north, skirting the massive butte, Ransom called a halt. He peered over his shoulder and nodded. They were out of sight from Faust and his men on the bluff at Narrow Gorge.

Wiping dust off his face with a bandanna, he explained to Rory and the women what he and Darby had learned. 'So, I'm aiming to climb up into the basin from this side. A mite harder, I reckon, but it can be done. I won't be asking any of you to join me. Best if you head back to the engi-

113

neer's camp on the river.'

Emma stood up in the buckboard and shielded her eyes from the sun. She studied the rock formation. 'You'll need all three lariats, Sam.'

'Probably, but—'

'But nothing,' Emma interrupted. 'I know Rory wants to go with you, but he's afeared about leaving me behind.'

'That's about the size of it, honey. I'm torn in two.'

'Well, you can patch yourself up right away, dearest. I'll be joining you and Sam.'

'*What?*' Rory pointed at the seemingly sheer rock. 'You can't be serious!'

She folded her arms. 'If Sam goes, you should go, since you're his friend. And if you go, I go too.'

Abigail reached up and tugged at Emma's shirt sleeve. 'Is this wise?' She glanced away at her husband Darby then at Ransom. 'Remember what that engineer told Darby and Sam. We can't risk getting caught in there when—'

'I've already told you, I'm going alone,' Ransom said. 'Thanks for worrying on my behalf. And thanks for coming this far. It's my family those swine are holding. I've gotta go, no matter what that chief engineer says.'

Rory swung his horse alongside Bodie. 'I'm going with you – and so is Emma, it seems.'

Ransom shook his head. 'No, friend, your hands aren't up to it. I don't want your death on my conscience.'

Laughing, Rory thrust out his prominent chin. 'It's my decision, not yours. Your conscience doesn't enter into it, friend.'

'Oh, all right.' Ransom turned to Darby and Abigail. 'If you both go to the engineer's camp and see about delaying the deluge, that would be a great help.'

Darby shook his head. 'That Faust guy seemed a standup

114

sort of fellow, Sam, but he isn't going to listen to us. He gave fair warning. You know he'll go ahead, regardless. Besides, you need my gun to back you up.' Unspoken was the obvious truth that Rory's arthritic hands meant that he wasn't going to be of much help if things turned sour and a gunfight started. Darby looked at Abigail and after a moment she nodded.

Removing his hat, Ransom wiped his brow. 'I've known you all for many years and I must say you're the most awkward, annoyingly contrary bunch I've ever come across. True friends!' He grinned, and wheeled his horse round to face north. 'Let's go climb that little rock.'

CHAPTER 13

OLD GUNS

Gideon Meak led the way into the town from the eastern end. 'Over here,' he said and strode towards the livery stable.

Charlotte's heart sank at sight of the familiar building. For about two years after her ordeal, she'd had nightmares in which the livery stable had been oppressive yet unchanged. Now, the daylight reality showed that the place was much more dilapidated; several wall panels had come adrift and gaps were visible. The sign's paint was almost entirely erased, just the 'Eid' and 'ery' remaining. A chilly sensation crawled up her spine as Justus Meak shoved her inside. Perhaps the chill emotion wasn't fanciful. It was pleasantly cooler in here. The transition from intense sunlight to shade was stark and abrupt. And very welcome.

It took her a few moments for her eyes to adjust to the subdued light.

'Right, tie them up!' Justus said.

'What about . . . natural functions?' Charlotte ventured.

'Ma. . . !' Even in the poor light, Jane's flushed cheeks

were noticeable.

'I'm just being practical,' Charlotte said.

Gideon swore and strode out. Justus said, 'OK, you can have a leash.' He signed to Turner. 'Tie them real tight, but let them have about five feet of loose rope so's they can wander over there.' He pointed to a stall, its floor spread with straw.

'Sure.' Turner nodded and grinned, his lignite eyes burning into Charlotte.

When he'd finished tying up Charlotte and Jane, Turner made his way across the main street and entered the Cavendish Hotel. The staircase was rickety but it held his considerable weight. He climbed up to the roof and then stopped to swallow a gulp of warm water from his canteen. He leaned his rifle against the stone parapet wall and looked out: he had a good view on all sides. Feeling a little like a king might feel, he sat on the parapet with his Merwin Hulbert revolver resting in his lap.

He was glad of his sombrero, as the heat was intense up here. And there was no shelter. He felt sure that his drink of a few seconds ago was oozing out of him as he sat. He wondered if there'd be any liquor below, in the hotel. He was going to get very thirsty on lookout duty.

Then he smiled. The compact shape of Wade emerged from The Whiskey House Saloon, and his face was like thunder. Guess there ain't no booze in there, Turner thought, and chuckled.

As the day lengthened, the heat increased. Must be the hottest yet. Gideon Meak had ransacked The Real Golden Nugget Saloon from top to bottom and found nothing. Breaking furniture and mirrors had been most pleasurable, however. But right now he wasn't feeling any pleasure, only frustration. He burst through the batwing doors, and as soon as he stood on the boardwalk in the direct glare of the sun, sweat dripped from every pore.

His muscles ached and his mouth was dry. He felt angry and annoyed. He didn't know whether to curse Ransom or his pa.

Suddenly, he stopped.

Movement to his right – by the assay office. Opposite the livery stable.

He pulled out his Colt Model P revolver. Surely that wasn't Ransom?

He glanced around, but he couldn't see any sign of Justus or Wade. From here, he couldn't see the roof of the Cavendish Hotel – it was only next door – so he couldn't attract Turner's attention either. He'd have to investigate by himself.

'Hey, anybody there?' a voice called.

Interesting. Not Ransom, then. He wouldn't be so incautious.

Gideon stepped out into the centre of the main street, his gun held behind his back. 'Who is that?' he shouted.

A man in overalls clambered down the steps from the boardwalk outside the assay office. 'Hey, there, glad I've caught you.' He seemed unarmed. 'I'm sorry to say, but you're trespassing!'

'Really?' Gideon said, strolling towards the man. He holstered his six-gun.

'Name's Algy,' the stranger said. 'I've been sent by the project's chief engineer.'

'Chief engineer?' Gideon smiled. 'Is that so?'

'Yeah, we saw your horses in our corral. Didn't you read the notice?' He was about two feet away.

Closing the distance, Gideon shook his head. 'Sorry, must have missed it.'

'I guess so. I've got to take you out of here. I need to get all you folks mustered together so we can leave the basin pronto.'

'Why the haste?' Gideon asked, fingering the knife on the belt at his back.

'We're flooding this whole basin tomorrow.' Algy stopped in front of Gideon, his hands on his hips, and glanced left and right. 'Where are the rest of you? Seven, we reckon.'

'No, there's only six of us.'

'We counted seven horses.'

'One of our company died.'

Algy grunted. 'Oh, sorry to hear that.'

'Yes, he died from a fatal stab wound – like this.'

Abruptly, Gideon pulled out his knife and thrust up, the blade penetrating under Algy's chin.

Algy stared. He gurgled his surprise and fell backwards, dead.

Gideon knelt down and retrieved the knife. He wiped the blade on Algy's overalls and then he smiled, his mood somewhat improved. As he dragged the body up the steps and dumped it inside the assay office, he hoped this business could be over soon, and then he could use his knife on the two women. Justus had promised; well, sort of promised.

When they reached the base of the rock face, Darby said, 'Why can't we just wait till night and use the goat track?'

'They'll be expecting us to come that way,' Ransom explained, tying Bodie to the rear of the buckboard. He unfastened his spurs and then straightened and looked at the jagged surface that stretched high above. At least it wasn't as sheer as it first appeared from a distance. There were plenty of ledges and handholds. But it was a long way up.

He put the spurs in the back of the buckboard. 'Are you sure about this?' he asked the women as he withdrew his rifle from the saddle scabbard and looped his lariat over his shoulder.

'Sure I'm sure,' Emma said.

'Yes,' Abigail said faintly, clasping Darby's hand.

'All right, then I'll go first.' He gestured at the lariats they held. 'You're responsible for each other.'

Darby was roped to Abigail, Rory to Emma. Watching them, he said, 'I'll rope myself to Charlotte when I rescue her.' It seemed the thing to say; but there was an awkward silence. He broke it: 'See you at the top.'

Darby, Rory and Ransom hung their rifles on their backs. Ransom turned, strode to a cluster of boulders and jumped onto a big rock, landing with his good leg first. His gloved hands snagged an outthrust chunk of stone and he used it for purchase to heave himself up. A few pebbles scattered under his boots, then he was on his way.

He reckoned that in ordinary conditions the rock climb would be difficult for people of their age. But in this heat, it was fearful. Yet at the outset, it hadn't been so bad. Sure, his leg gave him grief, but he was used to that. Then his joints started aching and his muscles straining. Those bruises seemed to resurface, reminding him he was no longer a young gun any more. As if he needed reminding. He pursed his lips. Yeah, we're all old guns, sure enough. A generation had gone by since we did anything like this. Maybe it wasn't such a good idea to go against those young guns? Maybe. But he wasn't left with much choice.

About a third of the way up, he paused on a narrow stone

shelf and glanced over his shoulder at the others. He shouldn't have let the women come. Hard to stop them, though. They were as stubborn as their husbands. He smiled, thankful that he had such staunch friends.

Now Darby was close, Abigail not far behind him. It looked as though Rory was having problems. Probably his hands couldn't easily grip hold. Ransom bit his lip. Too late to go back. He turned and started to climb again.

He hadn't got much further when abruptly a bird flew out of a dark crevice, its wings and feet scattering dust and pebbles. Startled, he lost his grip. His stomach lurched and he was sure his heart leapt into his mouth as he fell.

Darby's hand grasped Ransom's arm and arrested his fall.

Ransom hit his left shoulder against the rock face. Jarred, but undamaged. Another bruise to add to the others, that's all. His heart pummelled at his chest wall.

'Sam, you all right?' Darby asked.

Hands scrabbling for a firm hold, Ransom wheezed, 'Yes, thanks.' He glanced at Darby. His friend had looped the rope round a rock for support, to stop Ransom pulling him and Abigail down. 'That was quick thinking.'

'Just don't do that again, eh?' Darby massaged his right shoulder. 'You're carrying a lot of weight these days.'

Ransom laughed. 'You're worse than Charlotte, with your nagging!'

'Be careful, Sam,' Abigail said. 'I'll tell her what you said when we see her!'

'Yeah. Well, thanks.' His heart rate having slowed a little, he resumed the climb.

He was glad of his hat, as the sun beat down on him, intense, sapping his strength. He marvelled at the women. Well, they were both younger than him by several years.

Must stop making excuses, blaming my age, he thought. Thinking about Emma and Abigail, he couldn't avoid dwelling on Charly and Jane. God, he'd better be in time!

'Time for grub,' Gideon said. 'Here, make yourselves useful.' He beckoned to Charlotte. 'Cook us some bacon.' He dropped a saddle-bag on the straw-littered floor of the stable.

'Only if you give us some water,' she croaked.

His face suddenly flushed, Gideon stepped over the saddle-bag. 'Why, you bitch, you don't give me lip!' He raised a fist.

'Leave her be, brother,' snapped Justus, thrusting a restraining hand out. He turned to Charlotte and flung a canteen to her. 'You can use the blacksmith's fire,' he said, pointing to the stone construction at the right of the front doors. He flushed out a box of Lucifers from his vest pocket and tossed them over.

'Thanks,' she acknowledged begrudgingly.

'Clang that anvil when it's ready,' Justus said and left with his brother.

Swaying on her feet, Charlotte opened the canteen and lifted it to her lips. The water was warm and slightly salty; she gulped, spilling a few drops on her chest. She stopped and went over to Jane.

'Here, darling. Taste nectar.'

'I don't want anything from those bastards,' Jane said.

'Please. We've got to keep up our strength.'

'Why? So's they can . . . they can. . . .' She broke down and Charlotte hugged her, soothing her. No matter how old her children might be, it pained her to see them upset. Her heart turned as she hoped Adam was all right.

When Jane seemed to have cried some of the hurt and

fear out of her system, she accepted the canteen and took two gulps of water. She wiped her mouth with the back of her hand and smiled. 'Thanks, Ma.'

'Let's cook,' Charlotte said, and her stomach rumbled, as if reacting even to the thought of food. They both laughed, if briefly.

Charlotte got up and rummaged inside the saddle-bag. She found a skillet, a dozen or so rashers of bacon wrapped in greaseproof paper, a couple of loaves of corn bread and two cans of beans. She licked her lips. 'Let's get that fire started.'

Wade checked out the ironmonger's in about a half-hour flat; there were no suitable hiding places. The floorboards were all secure, too, even for an aging place. He sneezed, dust he'd disturbed obviously an irritant. He stepped out onto the boardwalk. He was parched, but the canteen didn't do any slaking of this particular thirst. He needed a real drink. He shielded his eyes from the sun with a hand and peered up at the roof cornice of the Cavendish Hotel. Blasted Turner got the easy job, keeping watch – if he hadn't dozed off. Wade had to go from ramshackle place to place, hunting for a needle in a haystack!

Next, the general store. He smiled. Maybe there was a bottle or two of spirits here? He kicked down the door and the tinkling bell clattered to the floor. 'Shop, anyone?' he called.

No answer. He grinned. Get a shock if there had been, eh?

Many of the shelves had collapsed, while others bowed under the weight of unsold produce. Mainly air-tights. No bottles, he noted glumly.

He walked round the counter and stepped into the back office.

A dust-covered desk, with drawers, beckoned. He opened a drawer and whistled. At last! Turley's Mill Whiskey, no less. Quality wheat liquor and only half consumed, too.

He used a bandanna to wipe sweat off his brow and then dusted the seat of the chair behind the desk. He sneezed again and then tested it for sturdiness. It seemed substantial enough. He sat down, pulled the stopper on the bottle and guzzled a searing mouthful.

As the firewater hit his stomach and set his temperature rising, he rested his feet on the desk; his stovepipe boots needed a good clean. When they'd shared out the loot, he promised himself he'd get a servant to clean his boots every day. But was there any loot? Maybe it was a wild goose chase, like the Ransom woman said?

He rested the bottle on the desk, dipped into his vest and took out one of his stogies. He dragged a Lucifer against his boot, lit up and sucked in the smoke. Yeah, that's better. He was hot, aching and tired. But by God the whiskey and the cigar injected new life into his bones. All he needed now was a good woman – or a good bad woman, he allowed, chuckling.

After a couple of drags on the cigar, he gulped another measure of the golden liquid. He held up the bottle to the light that slanted through a gap in the office wall; the liquor glistened. He sure hoped this wasn't the only gold he'd find in this here town.

The five of them sank to their knees at the top of the ridge. Ransom felt all in and gasped for breath. He sipped at his flask of brandy and the fiery liquid seemed to reinvigorate him, even though he knew the effect was only temporary.

Uncomplaining, Rory nursed his arthritic hands, while Emma kneaded his shoulders. 'This'll get some of the kinks out, darling,' she said.

'If only your loving ministrations could work on my hands.'

'Hey, you've done all right,' said Darby, lighting a match and raising it to his quirly.

'Darby, better douse that cigarette,' Ransom said. 'I'd dearly like to smoke a cigar, but I don't want to risk the light being seen.'

'Yeah, Sam, you're right – as usual.'

Over to their right were the rising mountain slopes. And the ridge they were on formed a natural dam against the river Buroak that flowed down through the tumbled boulders, descending over to the southeast. Ransom pointed. 'That's where the water's coming from to fill the basin.'

'You reckon?' Darby said, glancing around.

'How are they going to do it?' Rory asked.

Ransom shrugged. 'Dynamite, I guess.'

'Oh, look!' Abigail pointed to their left.

Over the bluffs that loomed blackly on both sides of the blocked entrance, the sun streaked the sky with deep shades of red and orange. Thin grey clouds were edged with pale silver and pink. 'Isn't it magical?'

'Surely is,' said Emma.

'It's going to get cold up here,' Ransom warned them, even though the day's heat still radiated from the rocks. 'So try to keep warm.' He flicked open his fob. 'I'll take the first watch, then Rory, then Darby. OK?'

'Sure,' said his two friends in unison.

Not without envy, he watched them snuggle close to their wives for added warmth.

'First light, we go in,' he said.

'I'm sure that's what you said the last time, all those years ago,' mused Rory.

'Could be,' Ransom said. 'Seems like the past is catching up with all of us.'

CHAPTER 14

BAIT

As the time passed, Charlotte's eyes grew heavy with the waiting. She was glad that neither Wade nor Turner had been left to guard her and Jane overnight. Both men were built big and powerful. The twins had agreed to share the duty, Justus first. A single oil lantern hung from a wall hook, its wick turned down low. She lay on the straw and let Jane sleep. She pretended to sleep, and waited for Justus to be relieved by his brother.

Finally, she was rewarded when Gideon entered the stable and shook Justus. 'Go and get some more shuteye, brother,' Gideon whispered.

Justus moaned and sat up. 'Wasn't asleep. Just resting my eyes.'

'Yeah. No problem.' Gideon thumbed at her and Jane. 'The fillies're asleep anyway.'

Charlotte smiled to herself. And waited.

Eventually, Gideon leaned against the stable wall and dozed, his head slumped forward. This was the time to risk it. Gently, she shook Jane awake, her hand over her daughter's mouth. 'Get ready,' she whispered.

Already primed earlier in the day, Jane nodded.

Together, they stood, looping the loose length of rope that tethered them to the upright posts of the stall. Treading carefully, they moved as one toward Gideon Meak. He let out a sniffling snort and their steps faltered.

Charlotte stood still and prayed.

He didn't wake.

Swiftly, she looped the rope round Gideon's neck, tugged harshly and the other end tautened on the stall's corner post. Gideon woke instantly and his eyes started from his head.

'His gun, quickly, Jane!' Charlotte shouted, straining her arm muscles to keep the rope stretched tight.

His hand scrabbled for the weapon but Jane kicked it away and withdrew the six-gun. In the buttery light, her face seemed pale, her face fear-filled. Two-handed, she lifted the gun.

Gideon made sickening choking noises. His complexion seemed darker, his eyes staring.

'Let my brother go,' said Justus from the doorway, 'or I'll kill your daughter.'

Jane swung round, raising the six-gun.

Justus brutally kicked the gun out of her hand. 'Do it, now!' he shouted.

Charlotte let go and her stomach churned in fear of the inevitable retribution.

Coughing and massaging his throat, Gideon rose to his knees. He wheezed in air and glared up at Charlotte.

'That was a bad move, ladies,' Justus said. 'I'd thought of letting you go, after we'd done for your man. Now, I reckon I've got no choice. I'll have to give you to my brother.'

Gideon unsheathed his knife and stood. He grabbed

Charlotte's arm, his teeth clenched in a snarl.

'Steady, brother, I want them both alive for tomorrow.'

'I don't have to kill them,' Gideon rasped. 'Just hurt them some.' He flicked the blade at Charlotte's dress and her collar was sliced away and fell to the straw floor. Her throat pulsed. 'I need to spill some blood!'

'No!' Justus barked.

Holding the point of the blade against Charlotte's cheek, Gideon whined, 'Why not?'

'Once you've spilled blood, brother, I don't reckon you'll be able to control yourself. And I don't want two dead women on my hands – just yet, at any rate.'

'You ain't going soft, Justus, are you?' Gideon said.

'I don't hold with killing women, you know that.' He let out a harsh laugh. 'In their case, though, I'll make an exception – tomorrow, not before.'

Thursday, 21 July

Six a.m. Dawn sunlight spread over their camp. Ransom unkinked his muscles, though not with complete success. His game leg was still stiff. Easing himself off the ground, he delved into his vest and checked his pocket watch.

Darby's face appeared morose as he passed him a tin cup of hot coffee.

'Thanks,' Ransom said. 'Quiet night?'

Nodding, Darby hunkered down by the small fire in a hollow and poured another cup. He straightened and handed it to Rory, still without speaking.

It was so long ago, but he recalled that Darby was always like this before a battle or a showdown. He sighed. We each have our own way of dealing with the close proximity of death.

The two women slowly roused themselves, peeling back their blankets. Abigail glanced at Ransom and shivered, though it wasn't cold.

'Let's get down there,' Ransom said, kicking dust onto the fire. 'We want to be in place before they set up any sentries.'

'I want to be lookout now,' said Wade as he finished his plate of bacon. 'It's my turn. I'm sick of digging around this dust-infested place. I've got a chest full of dust already.'

'All right,' said Justus. 'You two can switch. Wade, go on the roof of the hotel. You know where we came down, so that's where they'll come. When you get the first sight of them, let off two shots and we'll stop our search. Turner, you can search the remainder of the north side of the street. I'll do the rest of the buildings behind the main street; there's only a couple left.'

'OK, I'll check the western end of town,' Gideon said. He turned to the tethered women. 'What about them?'

Justus smiled. 'We set them where they can be seen. Any shooting starts, they get it first.'

'Seems a waste, to me,' Gideon said.

'I don't reckon Ransom and the others will risk their lives. They'll come peaceful.'

'Don't bank on it,' grated Charlotte.

Gideon slapped her cheek. 'I've told you before about giving me lip! I've a good mind to gag you!'

'No, brother, we want them to be heard – as they plead for their lives.'

Seven a.m. Charlotte stood facing west on the dusty hardpan of Main Street, a lariat tied round her neck and both wrists and then stretched to either side – secured to the uprights of the Real Golden Nugget entrance and the General Store. The rising sun was already hot on her back and her neck and head seemed to burn. It seemed as if her entire body broke out into a sweat. Her legs trembled with fear and the exhaustion brought on by lack of sleep, while her shoulders ached with the tautness of the rope.

From here she watched her long shadow gradually shrink towards her as the minutes passed. Further along the street, Jane was similarly tethered, the rope stretching between Desiré's Den and a house opposite, next to The Main Saloon, at the far western end of the town. Jane faced her – and the sun – but Charlotte couldn't distinguish her features.

She didn't know how long she could stand like this. Yet she must try; if she slumped down, she'd probably dislocate a shoulder.

Through dry lips, Charlotte prayed for deliverance.

Bait. Her head ached at the thought. We're bait.

Ransom and Darby clambered down, traversing the sloping sides of the basin. Brush and stunted trees grew round the black mouths of the abandoned mines and served as cover.

Abruptly, Darby halted and pointed to the roof of the Cavendish Hotel.

Ransom extended his telescope and studied the rooftop. He lowered the spyglass and nodded. 'They're up early as well. Just the one on the roof. He's looking to the west, expecting us from there.'

'Can Rory take him?'

'Sure,' Ransom said, though he wasn't. He peered to their left. Rory was two hundred yards away, darting among the skewed crosses of the cemetery; he stopped and waved. Sam gave the danger signal and pointed to the hotel. Rory raised his Winchester in acknowledgement.

Behind Rory, some fifty feet further up, Emma and Abigail negotiated their way down, hardly visible at all as they slunk from one boulder or tree trunk to another. They carried Ransom and Darby's rifles.

None of them had so far raised a tendril of telltale dust.

Grimly, Ransom signed to Darby and they moved again, the angle of their descent bringing more of the ghost town into view.

'Oh, hell,' Darby moaned. He hunkered down behind a big rock. 'Now what do we do?'

Crouching beside him, Ransom heaved in a big breath and let out a deep sigh. Despite the heat of the morning, a chill ran through him. Charlotte and Jane were strung out to dry.

He twisted round, eyed the rising sun. It seemed like the hottest day they'd had so far, and it was still early. Unprotected, his women were going to roast unless he did something damned soon.

'Bait,' seethed Darby, slamming a fist on the rock. 'The bastards are using them as bait.'

CHAPTER 15

DEAD MEAT

Eight a.m. Justus strode through the relatively cool shadows of a print shop, out the back and crossed a narrow street. Opposite was an alley with a couple of derelict private houses, presently in shadow. He kicked in the door of the first. Fortunately, sunlight streamed in through the broken windows and roof on the east side of the building, enough to illuminate the place. Methodically, he searched all the empty rooms.

By now, he felt frustrated. This was their second day and they'd found nothing. Nothing but dust and decay. The loot had to be hidden here! Had to be!

He stepped over the busted door and exited the building. Even here in the shade at this early hour, he was sweating. The air was still, oppressive. He took three strides and entered the far corner house. Immediately, he sensed that this was different. Gut instinct, maybe. Light poked through a gaping hole in the roof; the top floor had collapsed, as had the floorboards on the bottom. In the centre of the living area's floor was a large hole, more like a wide

133

pit. His pulse quickened.

Carefully treading over the creaking floorboards, he approached the lip of the pit. It seemed deep, and shadowy. He eyed the far wall; thin sunbeams slanted between the wallboards. He skirted the pit and kicked viciously at the wall. Neglected and rotten, the boards splintered and he created a ragged opening. Sunlight streamed into the room and illuminated the pit.

He hurried to the edge. It looked like there'd been a mine tunnel beneath this house. Then he let out a chuckle. 'Well, I'll be damned!' Below, partially in shadow, lay the skeleton of a big man.

'Now, that's nice,' he murmured. 'Real nice.' Under the skeleton, the end of a gold bar glinted in the sunbeam. He wiped the back of his hand across his lips and his bristles rasped. Now he felt vindicated.

Painfully gripping his Winchester, Rory made it to the back wall of the assayer's. From here he had a view of about half of the livery stable's frontage. The memories flooded back, the heat and dust, the shooting and shouting, and the death of Forrest and Burnside. He glanced down at his aching gnarled hands. Then, he'd been a good shot and almost fearless. Now, he sensed fear soaking into him. Fear of death, probably. Sure, his bones creaked, as if in need of oil, and his rheumatism played hell with him, but he wasn't ready to die yet, by God. He was only sixty-four, damn it!

The next building along from here was the Cavendish Hotel. While it was his job to silence the lookout on the hotel's roof, he decided he'd better check the street first. Sweat poured off him. He swallowed, his mouth dry. He cautiously edged along the side. While he passed a window, he peered inside and started. A dead body lay on the floor

134

to the right of the front door. The man wore bloodstained overalls. Must be Algy, the engineer's man that Sam mentioned. Shaken by the immediacy of recent violence, something he'd steered clear of for many years, he took a hasty look round the corner of the assay office, into Main Street, and then sharply pulled back behind the wall.

At this angle, only half of the street was visible.

Charlotte was still tied in the middle of the road. He hadn't detected any other movement. But he'd only taken a fleeting look. Any attempt at freeing Charlotte would be spotted by the lookout. And where was Jane?

He had no choice. He must tackle the man on the roof.

Silently, Rory walked back round the corner and hurried to the rear of the hotel.

Fortunately, the windows and doors were either open or broken, so he had no difficulty getting inside.

As he stood in the hotel's rear hallway, he welcomed the sudden relief from the intense heat of the sun. The air was still oppressive, but the pounding in his head had ceased.

Now all he had to do was get upstairs to the roof without alerting the lookout. He rubbed his damp hands on his dusty pants and ratcheted a shell into the rifle's chamber. Then he walked along the passageway, hugging the wall, and headed for the staircase.

Ransom was close on Darby's heels. While Darby stopped at the back of the general store, Ransom went on, like a shadow, hurrying further along the rear of the buildings, towards the western end of the town: he was intent on freeing Jane.

He passed the back accesses of the butcher's, the hotel and the printer's and entered the rear door of The Main Saloon. Warily, his Remington clasped in his damp hand, he crossed the back room and entered the main bar area, all covered in dust and cobwebs. No footprints. Nothing and nobody stirred.

From the cracked front window he had an uninterrupted view of Jane tethered in the middle of the street. His heart lurched at sight of her.

Jane's eyes were shut, her face lathered in sweat, her blonde tresses clinging to the side of her flushed face. Her clothes were dirty and stained. She swayed slightly and he feared that she wasn't far off fainting. He was surprised she'd lasted so long in this heat.

Although his fatherly instinct was to rush out and cut her loose, he didn't move. He peered to the left and the right, but he could only see about halfway down Main Street. Nobody else in sight. That was suspicious in itself. Perhaps there was a second man on another roof?

He holstered his Remington and wiped his palms on his shirt. Where the hell were the kidnappers?

As Turner walked past the general store, he looked side-ways, to the left. The Ransom wife glared at him, defiant. She'd learn before much more time had passed, he reck-oned. Her clothes were already a patchwork of sweat stains. Turning his attention to the butcher's, he entered the dark confines. Last night, he'd smelled whiskey on Wade's breath. Bastard probably found some in the store. No point in checking the store now, though – he'd have stashed it elsewhere. Not going to find much in here, either.

At least it wasn't full of carcases. Dark streaks stained the butcher's block. A rack of meat-hooks hung empty, collecting cobwebs.

He lifted a hand to brush the hooks aside so he could enter the door into the rear office. Without warning, an arm lanced through the doorway and slammed down on his hand, impaling it on a hook. The point went right through, came out the back. Gagging with pain, Turner turned to the doorway, his mouth forming a yell of agony, and met the full force of a pistol butt on the bridge of his nose.

Slumping to his knees, his body jerked and the impaled hand tore open. Another scream formed on his lips but never exited as a boot slammed into his chin with such force that his neck broke.

Darby hefted up Turner and threw the body onto the butcher's block. Dead meat.

Nine a.m. On the roof of the Cavendish Hotel, Wade scanned the western end of the basin and the spot where they'd entered, over by the water tower. He took a swig of the Turley's Mill Whiskey and licked his lips. He reckoned Justus was wrong. Those old men weren't capable of climbing that there goat track, let alone putting up a fight. Maybe they'd just come in docile-like, and tell them where the loot was. And get a bullet for their trouble. He grinned and took another gulp. Easy, he cautioned himself, not much left.

He heard a sound and turned and dropped the bottle in surprise.

'What the. . . ?' An old guy running towards— In the instant that Wade reached for his Colt Lightning, the butt of Rory's rifle slammed into his face and he had a broken chin to match his broken nose. A couple of teeth flew out the side of a smashed mouth and his Derby hat fell to the floor.

Wade staggered back towards the parapet.

Gideon entered Desiré's Den and stopped in surprise. The centre of the room was a shambles. Worse than the other buildings he'd searched. The remains of a massive chandelier mingled with two skeletons.

Gingerly, he walked over and knelt down to examine them.

No telling how long they'd been here. Maybe they were men from Pa's gang?

He noticed a faint glint in the gaping mouth of one skeleton and he grinned. Unsheathing his knife, he prised loose two gold teeth. As he tossed them in the palm of his hand, he hoped this wasn't the only gold they'd find here.

Better continue the search, he thought, and shoved the teeth in his vest pocket.

Rory recognized Wade Ashby from dodgers displayed in Rapid City: *Gun-for-hire and bank robber.* Aware of the muscular size of his opponent, Rory rushed his advantage again. Before the gunslinger could recover, Rory swung the Winchester round, slamming it into the side of Wade's head, diverting his jerky movement away from the front parapet.

Hands hurting like hell, Rory clasped the rifle under his arm and kicked at Wade's hip.

Wade's legs buckled under his massive weight and he tumbled to the parapet at the rear. Another kick on Wade's ass and the man sailed over the edge.

Gingerly, Rory peered over the lip of the roof.

Wade lay twisted and broken, face-down on the ground.

Rory heaved in a great sigh of relief and nursed his pained hands against his chest. His clothes were soaked in sweat and it seemed as if every bone in his body ached. He dearly wanted to lie down and rest.

Slowly, he walked across the rooftop and hid behind the apex peak of the false front.

From here, he had a perfect view of the street.

His mouth went dry as he spotted Abigail and Emma skulking from the livery stable along the northern side boardwalk, closing in on the rope that secured Charlotte's right wrist.

Hastily, he scanned the rest of the street, but there was nobody else in sight – save for poor Jane, whose knees seemed to be giving out. He winced, imagining how painful that taut rope must feel on her arms.

Through narrowed eyes, Emma gripped Ransom's rifle and checked the street ahead as she crouched on the boardwalk outside the ironmonger's. Even at this time of day, the sun beat down on them with searing force. She was grateful for the rickety old veranda roof above the boardwalk. Still, it was terribly hot, the air uncomfortably close. She couldn't even guess how Charlotte and Jane felt. She glanced behind her. Abigail stood in shade with her back to the shop wall, her face pale, eyes fearful; she held her husband's rifle but Emma doubted if she was capable of using it.

Just a few paces more, and they'd be level with the rope tied to the veranda post.

Charlotte slumped, arms outstretched, her head lowered. All around her spots of sweat discoloured the ground.

Emma jacked a shell into the chamber and waited. Nobody reacted to the sound – not even Charlotte. For a fleeting moment, Emma feared for her friend. Then she stepped forward. 'Cover me,' she whispered harshly to Abigail.

'Right,' Abigail mumbled.

Two more paces and she pulled out the knife Ransom had given her. 'Charly's probably fed up with me rescuing her – you can do it this time,' he'd said.

She sawed the blade against the taut rope.

The motion alerted Charlotte and she looked up. She smiled and mouthed 'Thank you'. A bit soon, Emma reckoned. She isn't loose yet. If Charlotte's the bait, where's the kidnap gang?

Darby left the butcher's and, six-gun drawn, he stepped out the back. He emerged into a narrow street, familiar ground even after all these years.

He thought he heard sounds coming from the ruins of the private houses down the next alley, the same house where he'd found Jubal unconscious on top of the body of George Scott. He licked dry lips.

There wasn't any ghost waiting for him, he knew, but it felt a mite eerie to be here again.

Ten a.m. Emma cut through the rope and Charlotte let out a grunt as her arm flopped to her side. With immense relief, Charlotte swivelled round and took a few steps to her left to ease the tautness of the other end of the rope. She sank onto her knees, her wrist and throat still fastened to the rope.

Emma ran into the street beside Charlotte. 'Thanks, Em,' Charlotte croaked. Emma hastily unlooped the rope from around her friend's neck and then stopped, appalled by an urgent shout.

'Hey, what the hell you doing?' bawled Gideon at the other end of the street, as he emerged from the swing doors of Desiré's Den.

Through heavy lids, Charlotte watched as Gideon ran to her daughter's side. 'No!' she rasped as Gideon levelled his knife blade against Jane's throat.

140

Emma glanced at Abigail who held both rifles. It was too far to risk a shot, anyway.

Gideon shouted, 'Stop there – or I'll cut her throat!'

CHAPTER 16

REVELATIONS

Ransom recognized Gideon from Adam's description. Gideon's eyes were on Emma and Charly; this was the only chance he'd get. Ransom hurried in an awkward limping gait, through the doorway of The Main Saloon, both Remington six-guns drawn. Ignoring the pain in his leg, he moved as fast as his ageing body would allow.

Out of the corner of his eye, Gideon saw him coming, but his reactions were slower than a bullet. Ransom fired once, the slug slamming into Gideon's right shoulder.

Thankfully, the knife dropped from Gideon's hand. Wounded, bellowing in pain, Gideon twisted away, keeping the figure of Jane between him and Ransom.

Frustrated, Ransom limped to Jane's right side to get a better view.

Gideon fumbled with his left hand and pulled his Colt Model P from its holster. Shakily, he aimed at Jane.

Two shots from behind Gideon buckled his legs under him. Almost in the same instant, Ransom fired, his bullet hitting Gideon in the chest. He dropped the Colt.

142

As Gideon lay there, blood filled his mouth, pain etched into his face, and his eyes seemed to ask unanswerable questions.

Charlotte walked hurriedly and stood over him, the rifle barrel smoking. 'You hurt my son, you bastard!' Tears streaked down her powder-burned sweat-covered cheeks.

Ransom kicked the Colt away and took Charly in his arms. God, it was good to hold her. She was safe. Both of his women were safe.

'Pa!' Jane shrieked.

Ransom swivelled round, shielding Charly. Gideon had another knife and raised it to throw. Ransom fired, a head shot, and Gideon Meak fell dead.

Frustrated at not finding any more gold bars, Justus climbed out of the pit with his heavy single bar. The others weren't going to be pleased, if this was all there was to show for their efforts; still, if Ransom turned up, maybe he'd know more.

As he approached the door, a shot was fired. Must be Wade, he'd spotted Ransom coming – though it didn't sound like a rifle. At the door, he stopped as two more shots went off – definitely a rifle that time. And another shot. *What the hell's happening?*

He stepped out into the alley and another shot was fired – it came from Main Street.

There was the silhouette of a man at the end of the alley.

Instinct impelled Justus to change direction and run round the corner of the building he'd vacated. A pistol barked, the bullet clipping the side of the house. Splinters flew.

Damn, Ransom was here already! What was Wade playing at?

The gunshots had come from the western end of Main Street, he reckoned, so he'd run east, towards the livery stable. Maybe he could grab the Ransom woman as a hostage.

The weight of the gold bar affected his gait and he was sweating. Short of breath, he glanced behind him.

A man had turned the corner and now fired his six-gun again.

The shot was damned close; it clipped the brim of his hat. Too close.

Ahead was the back of a fancy building, looked like a whorehouse, with a couple of lean-to cots for the poorer clients. Beyond that was the livery.

He ducked into the whorehouse.

Standing in the shade of the veranda, Emma heard the shots in the parallel street behind Main. 'Sounds like Darby might be in trouble,' she said.

Tearfully, Abby nodded. 'He can take care of himself, Emma. Let's stay here.' It was plain that Abby was fearful – understandably – and didn't want to risk her life further.

Charlotte had taken Abby's rifle and summarily dealt with one of the kidnappers, Emma thought, and Sam had finished off the swine. Now Sam had his two women safe, Emma decided she must put some iron in Abby's backbone. Determinedly, she gripped her rifle and said, 'No, we need to go. Darby might need help.'

Reluctantly, Abigail followed.

They ran along the boardwalk, towards The Whiskey House. 'The shooting's behind here,' Emma said. 'Come on!'

They went inside and at the back door stopped. Emma peered out, but the alley was clear. Directly in front of her was a bordello, its huge shingle now cock-eyed: Rest Awhile.

Emma stepped onto the narrow boardwalk, climbed the entry steps and went in.

She moved through the tawdry lobby with its moth-eaten plush velvet couches and a long bar counter on the right. As she approached the back door, it opened and a man entered.

'Oh!' Abby exclaimed. Perhaps she'd been expecting her husband.

It wasn't Darby, so Emma raised the rifle and snapped, 'Hold it right there, buster!'

11 a.m. Darby entered a few minutes later, his six-gun raised and cocked. He noticed a man sitting on a settee, his hands raised, and the gold brick by his side. Emma had her rifle levelled on him.

'He says his name's Justus Meak,' Emma said.

'Let me at him!' Darby snapped, stepping forward, gun raised.

'No, Darby, we should take him in,' Emma said.

'After what he and his gang have done?' Darby shoved his hat off his forehead with the end of the Colt barrel. 'They killed Jubal and Abner, that we know of, and seriously wounded young Adam!'

'We aren't the law, Darby.' Emma moved a step to one side so she could cover both Justus and Darby. Abigail stood frozen, eyeing them both. 'You know that,' Emma said.

'Of course he knows,' Ransom said as he walked in. Behind him was Jane, supported by Charlotte and Rory. Slung over Rory's shoulder was a thick coil of rope.

Darby shrugged and holstered his gun. 'Yeah, I know.'

Ransom stepped up to Justus and pointed at the gold bar. 'Where'd you get that?'

Scowling, Justus said, 'Your wife, she was telling the truth, wasn't she? There ain't no loot here, is there?'

'Not that we know of,' Ransom said. 'We searched, sure, but didn't find any.'

'I found that bar under a skeleton,' Justus said. 'The floor of a house caved in.'

'Yeah, I know the house. Mine tunnels underneath.'

'That's it,' said Justus.

'And only the one gold bar, under the body, is that right?'

Sourly, Justus nodded.

Ransom turned to Darby. 'Can you explain that?'

'Me? Why would I explain it?'

'You found Jubal unconscious on top of Scott. You were away from us for a while and, by the time you found us, you were helping Jubal walk since he was still very dazed. In fact, his memory was never the same again, was it?'

'Well, yes,' Darby said, gesturing vaguely, 'you know that, Sam.'

'Where's this leading?' Abigail asked tremulously.

Ransom sighed. 'Somewhere I don't rightly want to go, Abigail.'

Darby sat down opposite Justus and put his head in his hands. 'But he has to go there, Abby.' He peered up at Ransom. 'You have to, isn't that right?'

Nodding, Ransom said, 'You might as well tell us.'

'All right.' He glanced at his wife and she turned away. His face frozen, he looked at the others. 'What I said was true enough. I found Jubal lying on top of Scott at the bottom of the hole in the floor. It was obvious, they'd tussled on the floor and it had collapsed under them, into the mine tunnel.' He wiped a hand over his sweating face, and then dried it on his shirt. 'The dust had barely settled when I got there. All around them was the gold bullion – fifteen bars. Brax must've hidden it there. So, I hid it in another nearby offshoot tunnel. Then I carried Jubal out and revived him. I didn't tell any of you, naturally.'

'Naturally,' Ransom said.

'Damn.' Justus Meak groaned. 'That explains the gold bar under the skeleton . . . Scott.'

Darby nodded. 'I must've missed that one. I came back for the hidden gold some weeks later,' he explained. 'I told Abby what I'd done. Hell, I felt guilty about taking it, of course. I'd been straight all my life; well, mostly. We agreed I'd use the money to finance the building of a school. And I bought a printing press and went into business. I always regretted it, but I convinced myself that good had come from my actions.'

Ransom took a step closer. 'You saved my life during that climb, Darby. But—'

'I know, it was stolen bullion; it didn't belong to me.'

'It was a long time ago,' Abigail pleaded.

Darby stood up, adjusted his gun-belt. 'I can't go to prison at my age, Sam.'

Ransom stepped back. 'I take your meaning, Darby, but after all these years it might not come to that.'

Darby's eyes never left Ransom's. 'I never thought we'd have a showdown between us, Sam.'

'Me neither.'

Emma grabbed Ransom's arm. 'Please, stop it, you're both too old for all this!'

CHAPTER 17

WALL OF WATER

Noon. On time, several explosions went off, echoing around the basin. Ransom pulled out his fob. 'Hell, it's time!' He turned to Darby. 'This can wait – let's get out now!' He noticed Darby shove the gold bar inside his shirt, but it wasn't the time to protest, as water gushed up through the floorboards, like thousands of small geysers.

By the time the eight of them reached the front door of the Rest Awhile bordello, they were all soaked. Though alarming, Ransom welcomed the coolness of the water, a change from this infernal heat. They walked out onto the steps above the narrow boardwalk.

'I think the water's coming up through the mine shafts!' Charly said.

'My God, will you look at that!' Emma exclaimed.

The narrow back street was already under six inches of fast-running water.

'We need to get to high ground,' Ransom said.

148

'Top of the hotel!' Rory suggested. 'Its roof seemed solid enough.'

'No.' Ransom scanned the lip of the basin. No telling how high the waterline would be when the flooding stopped, but he remembered Mr Faust, the chief engineer, said the town would be buried under water. 'We've got to get out of this basin.'

'Where's all the water coming from?' wailed Abigail.

Ransom jumped into the swirling mud. The water was just below his knees. He braced himself against the strong force of it and limped out to the corner of the bordello. From there, he had an uninterrupted view of the eastern end of the basin. Brown and streaked with grey, water spewed out of the cave mouths. To their right, more or less where they'd climbed, a broad waterfall plunged into the basin, washing away trees with its force. And that wall of water seemed to be increasing in size – and headed their way.

'They've breached the ridge we were on,' he called back to them. Best option was to head for the south side of the basin, try to scramble up the bur oak slopes.

He returned to the Rest Awhile steps. 'Rory, have you enough rope so we can all be tied together?'

'Sure, Sam. It stretched all the way across the street.'

Jane shivered at the memory.

'Then, let's get going, *pronto*!'

Within minutes, the rope was secured round Ransom's waist, then after a length of about four feet, it was tied to Charlotte's waist, then Jane, Emma, Meak, Rory, Abigail and Darby.

Ransom stepped down and led them across the narrow alley, the water swirling up to his thighs now.

By the time they reached the back door of the Whiskey

House Saloon, water covered the floor of the place. At least there it was only up to his shins. Wood creaked and groaned under the force of the water that rushed past and pounded against the east side of the building.

Chairs moved across the floor as if propelled by ghosts. Using tables for purchase as he passed, Ransom reached the entrance. He glanced back. All of them were still with him, their faces grim.

Main Street seemed much worse. It was like a river in full flood. Brown, roiling, the water surged past. The supporting posts of verandas groaned and shifted. The odd tile fell from roofs. The buildings were old and dried out, probably not capable of taking much more of this punishment. Holding a trembling post to brace himself, Ransom stepped into the torrent. The water reached his midriff now. 'Keep together!' he bawled above the din of protesting buildings and the pounding water.

His lips curved sanguinely, as the irony wasn't lost on him: he'd been half-joking at the foot of the cliff, when he said he'd tie himself to Charly on their return.

Slowly, each step a risk, he led them across the street; his pace had slackened as his game leg weakened and pained him. Maybe it was the cold water, or the exertion. Fortunately, the initial gush of water had carried most loose things with it. To his right was a cluster of chairs, hitching rails, stray boards and trees piling up at the spot where Gideon Meak had died.

Finally, he reached the other side. Hotel Cavendish didn't offer much respite, however. 'I'm going down the alley!' he shouted back to them. He didn't want to be inside any building now, just in case it collapsed. He led them through the gap where small eddies of murky water congregated, and on their right an external staircase was already splintering, separating from the wall of the Real Golden Nugget.

Breathless, his legs aching, his chest heaving with the effort, Ransom emerged from the alley. Ahead should have been the pond, but now there was just a lake, a rising expanse of water. A few yards to his right, near the water tower, floodwater swirled in a kind of vortex. Maybe it was the underground stream that fed the pond; maybe it was more mine tunnels that had caved in. His heart lifted at sight of the dry ground further ahead on the slope between the bur oaks. 'Almost there!' he called.

For a moment, he stood at the corner, a hand pressed against the wooden wall, steeling himself for one final effort. He glanced left and right. He had to remember where the limits of the pond were. The water came up to his chest. He needed firm ground to walk on; if they had to swim, they'd be swept along to the western end of the basin, and risk hitting into any number of dangerous obstacles.

Straight ahead should be all right, he reckoned, signalling to the others to push on, his limp now more pronounced. From time to time, the rope tugged on his waist, but this was probably one of the others getting out of step or experiencing difficulty with the unpredictable eddies that seemed to hit without warning.

As he climbed the gradual slope, he noticed the level of water was lower on his body. Yet the tug on his waist rope seemed to be intensifying. He turned to look back at the others. At that instant, Abigail shrieked, 'Darby!'

And Ransom was pulled back, his feet sliding on the muddy scree. Frantically, barely maintaining his balance, he grabbed at the bole of a bur oak and clamped tight. His waist felt almost torn in two. Holding on, he watched the others in the line and realized what was happening.

Darby was being pulled into a big vortex of muddy water.

If it was a mine tunnel beneath them, the vortex would stop once the air pockets were filled. 'Hold on!' he shouted, realizing that it was a stupid redundant order. 'Charly, can you come forward,' he shouted, 'get hold of my hand?'

'No, I'm being pulled back!' she wheezed, fear in her eyes.

Ghoulishly, skulls and pieces of skeleton from the cemetery floated towards Darby, circling in the vortex of churning mud, foliage and wood.

'I can't fight it!' Darby called out.

CHAPTER 18

ABOUT THE PAST

'No, Darby, please, no!' cried Abigail.

There was the flash of a knife and the pressure on the rope subsided. Darby, together with several skeletons, was sucked into the filthy maelstrom.

No telling how long the whirlpool would persist, Ransom reasoned, so he clasped Charly's hand and continued to climb. He'd seen Rory pulling Abigail to him; she'd follow, despite her grief.

From above, to their right, a sudden loud screeching sound alerted him and he halted and turned, anxious. The water tower's trellis beams collapsed and the large wooden container crashed into the whirlpool, like an enormous plug. A tremendous upsurge of water washed against Ransom, and then the grasp of the vortex was no more.

Gasping in the severe heat of the day, he limped forward again, and the others followed.

A few minutes later, four burly men scrambled and pressed through the bur oaks, all of them attached to ropes. Ransom recognized one of them – Mr Faust.

'Here, give us your hands and we'll get you out!' Faust said, extending his arm to Ransom.

At the top, they all collapsed, sodden and dispirited. Ransom felt there wasn't a bone or a muscle that didn't ache.

'That was a darned fool thing to do, Sam Ransom!' barked Willis Hearst, striding up to them.

Forcing himself to his feet, Ransom extended his hand. 'Thanks for sending your men down for us, Willis.'

'Least I could do, once Mr Faust told me you were in the area. Fortunately, two of his men on the bluff yonder spotted people wading through the water that rushed through Main Street. Faust put two and two together and told me his fears.'

'Well, we're mighty grateful to the pair of you. Thanks.'

'But why'd you go, knowing we were going to flood the place?'

'I had no choice. It's a long story.' He peered at the blazing sun. 'I reckon we'll be dry inside ten minutes, judging by the heat today. I'd appreciate you taking us to your tent town first. Then I'll tell you everything.'

Ransom noticed Abigail's tear-rimmed eyes as she stared at him, sobs heaving her chest.

'Most of it is about the past and best buried and forgotten,' he went on, nodding to Abigail. He pointed at Justus Meak who heaved up a stomach full of dirty water. 'It has to do with that man abducting my wife and daughter. That's all.'

Despite her grief and the pain in her eyes, Abigail gave Ransom a thin smile of thanks.

'Well, of course,' said Hearst.

Mr Faust stepped forward. 'Any word about my man Algy?'

'Sorry, Mr Faust, he's dead – killed by this man's brother, I reckon,' Rory said, thumbing at Justus Meak.

Sunday, 24 July

Their journey back had been sombre, due to the loss of Darby. Distraught, Abigail was silent most of the time.

It was heartbreaking to learn that Adam would have to use crutches the rest of his life. But he put a brave face on it and said, 'It won't stop me riding. My horse can be my legs.'

Justus Meak was held in a Bethesda cell while the Ransoms and neighbours attempted to mend some of the damage caused during the siege.

When the parting finally came on the platform of Rapid City rail station, Abigail said, 'I want to thank you for not saying anything about . . . about what Darby did.'

Ransom took her hands in his. 'He saved my life twice out there, Abigail. It's the least I could do, to preserve his name. After all, he did a lot of good with his ill-gotten money.'

'He always regretted it, you know?'

'I'm sure he did,' Charlotte said. She hugged Abigail and turned to Emma. 'You'll look after her, won't you?'

'Yes, I'll stay until she's sorted things in Deadwood.'

Abigail held hands with both Charlotte and Emma. 'Thank you for being such dear friends. It's going to be hard, I know, but with your help and prayers, I'll come through this.'

Rory shook Ransom's hand. 'Are you dead set on doing this alone?'

Ransom exchanged a glance at Charlotte and she

nodded. 'I reckon you could've used a better phrase, friend,' he said, 'but yes, it's something that needs to be done.'

A siren alerted them that the train was approaching.

As Ransom steered Bodie on the approach to the ramshackle building, he glanced across at Justus.

Meak seemed to live up to his name since the flooding of the basin. During their ride here, the surviving twin had been no trouble at all; he'd hardly spoken.

The homestead was dilapidated – not much better than the ruins in that submerged ghost town, Ransom reckoned. A few hens clucked around, scattering as Bodie moved between them. A pig in its sty snorted. As a good neighbour said as he tended the livestock, 'The least I can do for an ailing old woman'.

At the hitching rail, Ransom dismounted. Then he helped Justus down; the handcuffs clinked.

'I really thought she'd be dead and buried by now,' Justus whispered.

'Yeah, and me with her, no doubt.' Ransom removed his hat and knocked on the door.

'Who's that?' a woman croaked.

'I've brought your son to see you!' Ransom shouted.

'Son?'

Gripping onto Justus, Ransom entered and the smell of the place hit him. The bed was on the left of the single room, occupied.

'Why'd you say "son"?' she asked, a fearful tremor in her voice.

Ransom shoved Justus ahead of him.

'Because he killed Gideon, Ma,' wailed Justus, rushing to the bedside.

'Oh, my God, no, not Gideon!' Scrawny arms clasped her son as he leaned over her. Then she pushed him away and stared at Ransom. 'You!'

'Hi, Mattie. It's been a few years, I guess.'

She glared, her mouth twisting, but no words formed.

'I'm sorry you're ailing.'

'Sorry? What a nerve! I've hated you for making your life a success while mine's always been spent hiding from the law!' The strength of her vehemence took Ransom aback.

'Why didn't Brax use the money he stole from the rest of us? There was plenty. He didn't need to lead the life of a criminal.'

'He gambled it away, spent it on foolish schemes.' She spat on the floor. 'He wasted it!'

'What money, Ma?'

'I'll tell you later,' Ransom said.

Matilda Meak sobbed. 'Yes, if you must know, Samuel Ransom, I regretted running off with Braxton.'

'Ma? You can't say that. He was our pa!'

'He was a no-good lying cheat, and he conned me!' She raised skeletal hands to her face and sobbed. 'Go away, Sam Ransom. I hate you!'

'Is that why you sent your two sons after me?'

Abruptly, her hand darted under her pillow and emerged, shakily pointing a six-gun at him.

Ransom snatched it from her with ease. 'Someone could get hurt with that, Mattie.' Her hands were cold, leathery.

Then, it was as though she'd only held on for this moment. She slumped on the bed, her eyes glazed. 'Rot in Hell,' she murmured in her dying breath.

'Ladies first,' Ransom said, and a cock crowed.

157

EPILOGUE

PENITENT

Monday, 25 July

'Thanks for bringing back my prisoner in person, Mr Ransom,' Warden Trent said as they sat in his office, both sipping a glass of whiskey.

Ransom smiled. 'He has other charges to face, but this is the best place for him till the trial.'

'I must say, Justus Meak seems a changed man.'

Ransom nodded. 'I think he's feeling sorry for himself. And he learned a few truths before his mother passed away. Made him a mite repentant.'

'Well, he was always the better of the two.' Trent patted a couple of newspapers on his desk. 'Your report says you captured him on 21 July.'

'That's right. Why?'

'Well, the papers say it was the hottest day for twenty-one years. People in the cities expired with the heat. Quite a death toll, by all accounts. Terribly hot.'

'It felt like it.' Ransom grinned. 'But not as hot as where his brother Gideon's gone.'